William Langland

Langland's Vision of Piers the Plowman

an English poem of the fourteenth century done into modern prose

William Langland

Langland's Vision of Piers the Plowman
an English poem of the fourteenth century done into modern prose

ISBN/EAN: 9783742867131

Manufactured in Europe, USA, Canada, Australia, Japa

Cover: Foto ©Andreas Hilbeck / pixelio.de

Manufactured and distributed by brebook publishing software
(www.brebook.com)

William Langland

Langland's Vision of Piers the Plowman

Langland's Vision

OF

Piers the Plowman

AN ENGLISH POEM OF THE FOURTEENTH CENTURY

DONE INTO MODERN PROSE

WITH AN INTRODUCTION

BY

KATE M. WARREN

SECOND EDITION, LARGELY REVISED AND CORRECTED

NEW YORK

THE MACMILLAN CO.

MDCCCXCIX

(

CONTENTS

————◦⦿◦————

PREFACE TO THE FIRST EDITION.

It is necessary to open the preface to this book with an apology. When I began the translation of *Piers the Plowman*, some time ago, Mr. Stopford Brooke kindly promised to write a short Introduction for it, and until recently the book has been advertised as having this preface from his pen. Unfortunately, a sudden and severe illness has prevented Mr. Brooke from fulfilling the promise made when in health, and the accompanying Introduction has been therefore supplied by myself.

This book has been prepared for an audience of general readers. It naturally does not aim at appealing to the circle who read the poem in the original ; nor has there been any attempt to adapt it to the requirements of those students who look upon English literature as a subject for examination to be " got up " from " set books." My rendering is not a line-for-line translation. But it has been prepared for an increasing number of readers who, without being scholars in Early English, are yet sufficiently interested in our early literature to wish to read *Piers the Plowman* for themselves, either as pure literature, or in order to find the social history in it. In connection with the teaching of English literature in schools, and with lectures of different kinds under the University Extension system, I hope the book may also be of use.

As to the translation, I have chosen a prose form for it, and my aim has been to shape it in the way that seemed most fitted to express the original of the fourteenth century, yet not so as to repel a modern reader by its archaism. On the whole the English of the Bible has been my model, with the addition, wherever possible, of alliteration. It is the prose into which Langland's poem most naturally falls. And there is a reason for this. Our present Bible is, to a certain extent, based on the Bible of Wyclif, and Wyclif was contemporary with Langland. The two writers were both familiar with the same national stock of words, phrases, and turns of expression ; moreover, the work of each was done for the people, and expressly intended for a strong appeal to them. Hence our Biblical English is perhaps the nearest we can approach, without becoming either obscure or over-quaint, to the English of the fourteenth century. Although, under these conditions, I have been reluctantly obliged to

discard many a fine old word dear to the heart of
the student of English, I have occasionally ventured
to retain in the text words and expressions which
are practically obsolete in modern English prose, or
obsolete in the sense in which I use them; such, for
example, as " gleed," " shrew," " I can no Latin,"
' an she would," and some others. But in every
case they are terms used by Shakespere, or by some
good Elizabethan writer, and a note of explanation
has been added where there seemed any doubt of
the meaning being understood. As a rule, then, I
have endeavoured to keep close to the original,
though at times, for the sake of clearness, I have
not hesitated to give a more general version of the
sense.

I have tried to make my rendering as accurate as
it can be. It is impossible, however, but that here
and there errors of translation will be found, and I
shall be grateful to any scholar who may feel suf-
ficient interest in the book to point these out.

The text of the *Vision* used as the foundation for
this rendering is that known as the B-text, pub-
lished by Professor Skeat in his small volume of
Piers the Plowman. [1] This text has also been
carefully compared with that in his larger edition
of the complete work, and occasionally the older
edition by Wright has been consulted. An occa-
sional reading has been taken from the C-text;

---

[1] *Piers the Plowman*, edited by the Rev. W. W. Skeat.
Oxford, Clarendon Press, 1891.

and an Appendix of the most interesting additional passages from the same version will be found at the end of this volume. The spelling of the mediæval Latin has been retained throughout. Only such Notes have been added to the book as are needful to bring out the complete meaning of the text ; and for many of these I am indebted to Professor Skeat's editions of the *Vision.* Readers who desire to know more concerning the points of history, archæology, and language connected with the poem are referred to these books, where they will find such matters treated with enthusiastic scholarship. [1]

And here I wish very heartily to thank Professor Skeat, who is always ready to help younger workers in his own field, for the very generous permission he has given me to make such use of his Notes as I have done. Without that permission my labour in annotating this translation would have been trebled. I would also gratefully acknowledge the cordial consent given to me for the same purpose by the delegates of the Clarendon Press, who publish the above editions of *Piers the Plowman.*

Finally, I offer my sincere thanks to the friends who have so kindly given me different kinds of help in preparing the book. Foremost among these is Mr. Stopford Brooke, who, in spite of illness, has

[1] *Piers the Plowman*, in three parallel texts, together with *Richard the Redeles*, edited by Rev. W. W. Skeat. Oxford, Clarendon Press, 2 vols.

read and criticised both my MS. and proof-sheets, and, I need not say, has made invaluable suggestions. I should also like to take this opportunity of expressing to him my gratitude for the enlightenment, inspiration, and pleasure that his fine criticism of English literature, in book and lecture, has given to me and to many other students both in England and abroad.

To Professor C. H. Herford, of University College, Aberystwyth, I am much indebted for reading parts of my proof, and for advising me upon several points of rendering at a time when his hands were full of other work. To Miss Toulmin Smith and Mr. Graham Wallas I owe thanks for other aid ; and I am also grateful to a fellow-student, who has been kind enough to revise my work with the original, and to make many a helpful suggestion. With these marks of good-will upon it I send the book forth, in the hope that it may be received with something of the same friendly interest by the larger world of readers for whom it has been prepared.

KATE M. WARREN.

January 14, 1895.

PREFACE TO THE SECOND EDITION.

———•◦•———

THE second edition of this book now issued has been revised and corrected. I wish to express here my gratitude to those various friends who have been good enough to send me suggestions for revision ; but more especially to Professor W. P. Ker, of University College, London, who has kindly given me a great many notes upon the book, and from whose lectures on Middle English literature I have also gained, as a member of his class, invaluable help.

KATE M. WARREN.

LONDON, *April* 15, 1899.

INTRODUCTION.

—◦◦—

WILLIAM LANGLAND'S *Vision of Piers the Plowman*
is one of the Early English poems that may well
appeal to many other readers than the professed
student of literature.   It will ever be attractive
to those who care for a vivid account of certain
phases of life in England at one of the important
periods of her social history ; but, beyond this,
Langland's work touches some of the keenest
interests of our own day.   In its picture of the
life of the labourer, and its protest against the
oppression of the poor by the rich and powerful,
it connects itself with that impelling desire for
social reform which, in many and various ways,
is now striving to express itself, not only in England, but all over Europe.   Again, the plain moral
purpose of the poem—to uphold the value of the
good life, and the evil of its opposite—links it
somewhat to the modern interest in ethics, while
the realistic treatment of certain portions of its
subject matter may commend it to the prevailing

taste of the day in literature. Moreover, the deep humanity and living earnestness of Langland's work cannot fail to be felt by every reader.

But, having said this, we have to recognise that, quite apart from the strangeness of the older language, there are certain difficulties which beset the ordinary reader who comes to the perusal of a poem of 500 years ago. Though much of the ground thought and feeling of it may be akin to those of our own time, yet the whole outward atmosphere of the world it represents is as widely different from our own as a primitive country inn from a colossal hotel in London. Five centuries of political, social, and moral change divide us from the England of the *Vision*, and perhaps no change is greater, nor more affects the common life of the people, than that which the lapse of years has brought about in the position and influence of the Church with regard to the whole of society. In the fourteenth century she was the overshadowing mother of the nation ; all but the most evil outcasts were included in her fold, her blessing brought prosperity, her curse ruin. Her servants were everywhere in society ; evil-doers they often were, but the worst of them was believed by the unlearned folk to possess a mysterious spiritual power, with which the Church had herself endowed him. And even those who saw clearly enough the abuses of the visible institution could still recognise that there was an invisible and ideal Holy Church, which, however unworthily represented on earth, yet justly claimed obedience and honour from all her children. More than anything else does this fact of the all-prevailing presence of the Church hinder us from realising fully the inward and outward condition of life in which our forefathers lived. And it forms one of the main difficulties to the reader who may take up *Piers the Plowman* for the first time. It is little wonder, then, if, when we turn to enter that bygone century, a mist of unreality should at first dim our vision of the real human beings who move throughout the book. But a slight knowledge of the history of the fourteenth century in England, and a little imagination, will go far to put us in sympathy with the world of Langland.

The *Vision of* (i.e., *concerning*) *Piers the Plowman* is only a portion of a much longer work known to students under its Latin title of *The Book of Piers the Plowman* (*Liber de Petro Plowman*). This "Book" describes a series of dreams or visions seen by its author, in which many allegorical figures. appear, and of all these personages Piers (or Peter) the Ploughman is the most important ; so that though he does not come into all the dreams, yet the book is named after him.

The complete set of visions falls into two great parts—the *Vision of Piers the Plowman*, forming about one-third of the whole, and the three-fold Vision of *Do-well, Do-better, Do-best.* The first of these is translated in this volume ; the second is, on the whole, of less general interest than the first. Passages of beauty and interest occur in it, but it is discursive, the narrative element is not so good as in the first, nor is the allegory as clear, and there is much moralising.

The whole work is written in alliterative verse, the form of metre in which nearly all our poetry before the Conquest was produced. After that event, however, this manner of verse almost disappeared [1] until the middle of the fourteenth century, when we have a revival of it in a group of poems, of which Langland's is one of the chief. It was not the most fashionable verse of the time, for that was French in manner, and was found in elaborate lyric metres or the short riming couplet, but it was English to the core, and would appeal very strongly to those classes of society beyond the circle of the Court for which Langland chiefly wrote.

Concerning the name of the author, though tradition and custom have tended to fix it in the form we here use, there is still some controversy. His Christian name, he himself tells us, was William, but whether his second name was Langland or Langley is not yet finally settled. The facts of his life are also uncertain. Some of these he reveals in his poems, but his parentage and ancestry, his date of birth, his birthplace, and his true position in the social scale, are undetermined,

---

[1] Some critics hold, and with reason, that it never really disappeared; but that we have lost what was written during the time.

though many sidelights are thrown upon them from the poems.[1]

The account of his life most commonly received, and that which Professor Skeat thinks the most credible, is the following. The poet was born about 1332 at Cleobury Mortimer in Shropshire. He was put to school, and became a scholar. When about thirty, in 1362, he wrote, perhaps at Malvern, the first draft of the *Vision* (known as the A-text). About 1377 he expanded this into a second and longer poem (the B-text), and at this time he may have been living at Cornhill, in London. A few years after 1390[2] he made the third and last revision of his work (the C-text), when he had perhaps left London. He seems to have been by profession a clerk of the Church, in minor orders ; but, for some reason, never rose to any high position in his calling, and only earned a fluctuating livelihood by such clerical duties as he could perform.

He was married, and from what he says, seems to have been often very poor. He probably wrote one other poem besides the great Book of Visions, that known as *Richard the Redeles*, in which he tells us that he was at Bristol in the year 1399. He was then perhaps about sixty-seven, and this is the last we hear about him.

From his own writings we know something of the poet's look. His tall stature was remarkable, so that people called him "Long Will." As a

---

[1] See especially Appendix, p. 121.
[2] M. Jusserand dates the C-text at 1398–9.

2

clerk of the Church he wore " long robes," and his head was shaven. His temperament made him moody, and perhaps his poverty made him proud. As he stalked grimly along the London streets he saluted no one, but he took notice of many a detail of dress and behaviour in the passers-by, which reminds us of Chaucer's habit of quiet observation. But with what different eyes the two men looked out upon the world ! There is hardly a more striking contrast in the history of literature than may be found in the life, character, mode of expression, and manner of work, of these two English poets, who lived perhaps within a mile of each other in the same City of London.

To discuss at any length the social and political conditions of that England of the fourteenth century to which these poets belonged, would alone need a volume, and in various ways it has been already done by writers of authority and insight.[1] Moreover, the poem itself gives no inaccurate account of many phases of social life in England. Langland's picture of priests, hermits, friars, lawyers, doctors; of the doings in the law-courts; of the various classes of labourers, minstrels, and beggars; of the fine lady, in the person of

[1] See Green's *Short History of the English People*, chap. v. ; *Town Life in the Fifteenth Century*, by Mrs. J. R. Green ; and M. Jusserand's *Piers Plowman : a contribution to the History of English Mysticism.*
Since the above was written a valuable book upon this subject has appeared in England : *England in the Age of Wycliffe.* G. M. Trevelyan. Longmans, 1899.

Meed ; of the sermon of an earnest-minded priest, in the preaching of Reason ; of the motley gathering in the inn ; of the cheatery of the retail-dealer ; of the lazy workman ; each and all are described from the actual life the writer saw around him, and are historically true. Still further, the spirit that was animating in different degrees the whole of society—the aspiration for a better social condition—finds an outlet in Langland's work. Our author gave voice to this widespread desire, not by advocating, with Wyclif, radical changes in church doctrine and church revenues, nor, with John Ball, a reorganisation of the order of society, but by demanding righteous dealing between man and man, in every class of society, in the Church, in the law-courts, in every kind of trade and labour, and in the everyday intercourse of common life. Langland sided with no particular movement or party : he is neither a Wyclifite nor a follower of the socialistic John Ball, nor is he in any sense a courtier. But he reproved and laid bare the injustice and evil-doing in every class—literally from the king to the beggar—and he favours none of them, except that by his choice of the honest ploughman as the type of righteous living he indicated, as other teachers of his time did, with what class lay the greatest hope for the regeneration of society. He was no democrat in social and political matters, though he touches the very germ of democracy when he says—a doctrine common to preachers :—

" In the charnel house at the church it is hard to know a knight from a knave." And that often quoted couplet, which not unfairly expresses, in a rude form, one of the human facts which is a foundation for democratic teaching, belongs equally to the teaching of Wyclif, John Ball, and Langland :

> " When Adam delved and Eve span,
> Who was then the gentleman ? "

But in his application of it he drew no partial or party inferences. He looked at all sides, and seems, therefore, at times, self-contradictory. But, as I have inferred, he is always consistent in the belief in Justice in the Platonic sense—each man looking after his own business.

He looked out upon a social organisation which was fast falling asunder ; for " the great fact of all modern history is the breaking up of the feudal and ecclesiastical system of the Middle Ages, and the introduction, as political and social elements of weight, of the middle and industrial classes." And in Langland's time we see the beginning of that process, in the Church, in political government, and in the organisation of society.

In the Church, we have a state of things which, of necessity, prefaces a change. What that state was the *Vision* itself plainly declares. It tells of a corrupt and selfish body of Church officials, of all ranks, from bishop to parish priest, who looked upon the Church as a means of getting an easy

Plowman. It will be remembered that the rendering in this volume only gives a portion of that *Book*—the *Vision* proper.

A brief analysis of the contents of the *Vision*, with a few comments, may be useful to the reader who comes fresh to Langland's work. The poem is divided into eight parts—a Prologue and seven other divisions, each of which is called a *passus* (or *portion*).

In the *Prologue*, the author falls asleep on Malvern Hills and dreams of an unknown wilderness, with a tower on the east of it, and a deep valley on the west, occupied by a dungeon. Between the two boundaries is a field full of people of all kinds, working or amusing themselves ; but the Church element, in one form or another, predominates. These are all more or less described, and none of them has a really good word from the poet, except the ploughman and the honest hermits. The narrative then slips off from the direct story of the dream into a further description of the doings of the Church dignitaries, and this leads to a digression upon the power of the keys deputed by St. Peter to the Church of Rome.

Then we are swiftly and abruptly transported back to the field,. into a group of which the king is the centre, and he is addressed by a lunatic, an angel, a " glutton of words," and the Commons. Then, all in a moment—and this is after Langland's special manner—the whole of this piece of action disappears, and its place is taken by a crowd of rats and mice, who come forth, helter-skelter, to a "council," and act out the fable of the attempt to bell the cat. This over, again the scene shifts to another quarter of the field, and once more we see the crowd moving hither and thither; and with the cries of the cooks and taverners of the street touting for custom, this portion of the dream closes.

Passus I. continues the vision. A lovely lady appears, and begins to tell the dreamer the meaning of all these things. The Tower is Truth, she says, and then she turns to speak of righteous living, but Langland interrupts her by asking to whom all the money of the world belongs. She answers him from the words of the Gospel, and goes on to explain what the dungeon in the valley means. The dreamer asks who this wise woman can be. She says that she is Holy Church; at which he begs her to instruct him, and the exhortation which follows, though in these days it may be considered an old-fashioned type of sermon, is full of common-sense morality put in vigorous phrase; and if it need an apology, we may ask a modern reader to remember its date, and view it from that standpoint. The " heavy " Latin sentences which interline it, and are found throughout the *Vision*, were not then a sign of pedantry, but represented to the hearers literal sayings from that Bible which few laymen of the day could read; and when they heard the Latin they felt they were getting the real thing, none the less efficacious

because they could not understand it. When
Chaucer's Pardoner preached, he tells us that

> . . . . in Latyn I speke a wordes fewe,
> To saffron with my predicacioun,
> And for to stire men to devocioun.

In *Passus II.* Holy Church is about to leave the
sleeper, but he begs her to stay and tell him more,
and especially to teach him to know "the False."
She points out to him Falsehood and his fellows,
and then follows the vivid description of Lady
Meed—the most subtly conceived personage in
the whole poem, a mingling of the legitimate
attractiveness of just reward and of the false
allurement of bribery—and the account of Meed's
approaching marriage to Falsehood; Holy Church
now leaves the dreamer, who sleeps on and sees
the preparation for the wedding of the two
deceivers. But Theology suddenly interferes,
reminding them all of Meed's rightful office; she
ought to marry Truth. He advises them to go to
the king's Court at Westminster, to get the matter
settled. They prepare for the journey and set off;
but when they arrive, being warned that the king
means to bring their ill-doing to justice, they all
disperse in dire haste, except Meed, who is
brought to the king. In connection with Meed's
trial, it may be remembered that, according to the
feudal custom, no heiress in wardship could marry
without the consent of her guardian, and Meed is
the ward of the king.

Passus III. shows us Meed at Westminster, lodged luxuriously until the time of her trial. She is so charming that every one wishes to be friendly with her. Judges and clerks visit her, and she gives them costly gifts. A friar hears her confess, and absolves her of her shameless sins, on condition that she pay the cost of a new window for their church, in which her name shall be engraven. This transaction calls forth a protest from the writer against such ostentatious alsmgiving.

We are then carried on to the trial of Meed, which extends to the end of *Passus IV.*, and is conceived throughout with a fine directness. The king would forgive the lady if she married Conscience. She is willing ; but Conscience scornfully refuses, and brings against her a long and vehement indictment. Meed asks humbly for leave to speak, and pleads for herself with such eloquent cunning that the king exclaims, " Meed, methinketh, is well worthy of the mastery ! "

Conscience, however, answers her, and shows the difference between the two characters involved in Meed—apparently denying to the lady before him any of the good qualities of pure Reward ; and he prophesies a golden age of Love and Justice. Meed, full of anger, attempts to open up a fresh dispute with Conscience, but the king silences them both, and tries to reconcile them. Conscience refuses to look at Meed unless Reason bid him. Then Reason is sent for, and comes to Court. The king pays him great honour, and they take counsel together. At this point there comes in—after that abrupt fashion of Langland, without any preliminaries—a plaintiff, named Peace, who presents a petition asking for redress against Wrong, who has used him ill. Meed tries to bribe Peace into silence, and Peace begs the king to stop the trial ; but this is refused, Reason supporting the refusal, and finally Meed is pronounced guilty and severely reproved by the king, who threatens that in future Reason shall judge every case in Court. Meed leaves the hall in disgrace, attended, however, by a sizer and summoner, and we see her no more. Reason agrees to stay with the king for ever. Thus ends the first dream in the *Vision of Piers the Plowman.*

We are now conducted to an altogether different scene, though the background of the action is still the Field of Folk. In *Passus V.* the dreamer awakes, but sleeps again, and sees Reason preaching in the Field before the king. Then there follows what M. Jusserand has finely called the " general confession of England in the time of the Plantagenets." Moved to penitence by the preaching of Reason and Repentance, the Seven Deadly Sins—Pride, Lechery, Envy, Wrath, Avarice, Gluttony, Sloth—make their confession, and it is a ruthless revelation of the seamy side of human nature in the fourteenth century. The subject is treated with the utmost realism, and it is in this portion of the poem that Langland most allows his grim humour to appear. But it is the stern humour of the Puritan, who sees judgment descending even as he speaks, and smothers his humour in reproof almost before it leaves his lips.

The confession over, Repentance prays for all the penitents, Hope collects them together with a blast from her horn, and they all set out on the famous search for the shrine of Truth. This is one of the best-known passages of the poem, and finely executed. There is strong pathos in the few lines which picture the blind groping of the pilgrims in their fruitless effort to find the right road ; and biting satire in the situation of the Palmer who cannot help them, though he has visited all the great shrines. Then, in the midst of their perplexity, with the weird suddenness already alluded to, Piers the Plowman comes forth, says that he knows Truth well, and will show them the way ; and his description of the road (which involves an interesting allegory) brings us to the end of the Passus, which concludes in a dramatic fashion with the sudden disappearance of a Pardoner to fetch his bull and brevets, as credentials on the journey, followed by a woman of ill fame, who would pass for his sister.

Passus VI. opens with the complaint of the pilgrims at the difficulty of the way before them ; Piers offers to go with them as soon as he has

ploughed and sown his half-acre. The pilgrims
in return offer to help him, and Piers, after making
his will, sets them all to work. At noon, going
to inspect them, he discovers many lazy vagabonds
taking their ease in complete idleness ; and this
gives the author occasion for a piece of satirical
and realistic writing of the same vigorous and
ruthless type as that which describes the confession of the Deadly Sins. After vain efforts to
make the loafers labour, Piers calls out for Hunger,
who cows them with hard usage, while in fear and
trembling they hurry to work. Piers gets some
useful advice from him, and would then bid him
farewell. But Hunger refuses to go, he must first
dine ; the people, in dismay, have then to feed him
with their scanty stock of provisions. Soon after,
a time of plenty comes to the land, and the Passus
·closes with a warning to the labourer against
reckless· indulgence of appetite in the year of
abundance, for Famine is always near at hand.

With *Passus VII.* we seem to lose sight of the
pilgrims, though we are still dimly conscious of
them in the background. Truth is now represented
as sending to Piers a bull of pardon for nearly
every class of sinner. Merchants and men of
law, however, are only partially pardoned ; false
beggars have no pardon. The allusion to beggars
leads the author to dilate upon the life and
doings of the numerous " bidders and beggars "
of the time ; by which we realise that in the fourteenth century they formed a complete "class."

Then a priest asks to see the bull of pardon sent to Piers, and finding in it only two simple lines— *those who do well, shall have well; those who do evil, shall have evil*—scoffs at it, when Piers in vexation tears the bull across, and the priest and he dispute upon it. Their contention awakes the sleeper, who debates with himself over the value and meaning of his dream. The *Vision* concludes with a fervent declaration concerning the efficacy of a good life, above that of all the Pope's bulls, at the Day of Doom.

It will be seen from this brief analysis that the poem falls into three parts—the account of the Field of Folk and its interpretation by Holy Church; the story of Meed and her adventures; and the confession of the Deadly Sins, together with the penitents' search for Truth and the final bull of pardon sent to them. All three are connected, but—and here lies the chief artistic fault in the work, too slenderly connected. A greater artist than Langland would not have been content to leave them thus; he would either have connected them more vitally, or else have kept them as three distinct poems. The scene of the three visions is supposed to be the same Field, but at times we forget that entirely, so little has it to do with the main interest of the narrative. Again, some of the same moral qualities are impersonated in different portions of the poem, such as Reason and Conscience, and might have served to link the whole together; but they are mere abstractions,

and not at all personages who exhibit any special
cast of character whenever they appear; they
only form a vital connection between the parts of
the poem in as far as they help to express its
unity of moral aim. It is therefore only when
we come to consider the separate dreams, and
particular incidents in the dreams, that we feel
justified in giving Langland much credit for his
literary form. The narrative of the Prologue and
of the Fable of the Rats, within the Prologue;
the whole story of Meed and each of her adventures; the incident of Piers and his doings
with the pilgrims, are all well and compactly
shaped. Skill in construction was not, then, the
strongest point of Langland; his strength lay
rather in his bold and vivid description of the
things he saw before him, in his narrative power,
in his direct, incisive dialogue, and in the language
and style in which he couched his whole work.

The chief element in his style is sincerity. This
reveals itself in passionate and rough directness,
in the uncompromising realism of his language,
and in a certain simplicity of dignity and manner.
As we read the *Vision* it is impossible to help feeling that Langland's aim in writing it was to
" deliver his soul." He did not make poetry for
pure pleasure. He had conceived, and passion-
ately loved, a high moral ideal for human life, but
he realised bitterly, looking on society, how far
short the actual everyday doing of men and
women fell of that ideal; and, brooding on this,

3

he was driven to express what he felt. Langland was an artist much in the same way as Bunyan was; the form of his work grew chiefly "out of passionate feeling, and not out of self-conscious art." What he had to say was more to him than how he said it.

But the allegory of Langland resembles Bunyan at other points. The allegorical things and persons have, to begin with, this important quality, that their allegorical character is clear; there is no confusion of allegory with reality. The Field, the Tower, the Dungeon, are on the surface simply allegorical. Holy Church, Meed, Liar, the Deadly Sins, Conscience, and the rest, are plainly allegorical too; we have no trouble in discovering whom they stand for. An exception may perhaps here be taken to the figure of Piers the Plowman himself. To our century he does not at once clearly represent an allegorical character, as in the case of Peace; but to the people of Langland's time he no doubt did. To them he must have been the type of Righteous Living—of the good life of *action*, lived in the world, as distinguished from the good life of *contemplation*, lived in withdrawal from the world, which was another thing altogether, and recognised as such.

We find, then, in the *Vision*, the first necessity of good allegory—to proclaim itself plainly as allegory. But there is another thing equally needful with this, the endowment of the allegorical machinery with life and human interest.

An allegory in which the scenes and figures are merely abstract virtues is as void of interest as the movements of automata set over against a background of painted trees. Bunyan's allegory is the very opposite of this, and so, too, is the greater part of Langland's in the *Vision.* Some of the figures are so human that we watch them with the same interest we should give to real persons. We follow the doings of Meed as if she were an actual woman and not a type of Bribery.

But this humanity of the allegorical personages does not belong to all of them. A careful observer will notice that it is the ill-doing folk in the story whom Langland makes most vivid; he describes them more fully than the others, he himself realises them more. To take but one example out of several, compare Holy Church with Meed. Of Holy Church we are only told that she was a lovely lady, clothed in linen, and of gracious speech. She is but a mouth-piece for moral and religious thoughts. We do not realise her as a woman. But look at Meed; her dress is minutely described, her charming manner, her plaintive and her angry moods, her triumphs and her distresses, her trickery and wanton ways—are cleverly indicated in a few touches, from time to time in the story. She represented in the main, to Langland, the most pernicious form of Self-Interest, but he saw her, too, as an actual woman, and so he makes us see her.

Even Piers the Plowman himself did not stand ⸺

forth in Langland's imagination as a vivid human being, like Sloth, for example. The poet could not realise the Ploughman as Bunyan realised Great-heart. The virtuous people in the *Vision* are rather reasoned out by the intellect than created by the vital shaping of the imagination from materials gathered out of real experience. And, in so far as this is true, Langland's work is less than Bunyan's.[1]

Langland's failure to realise in allegory the good as vividly as the evil seems to have sprung from the way he looked on actual life. It is true that the material conditions of life for a great portion of the population of England were unjust, cruel, and desperately evil. No one can read of that time without allowing this; but Langland fixed his gaze almost exclusively upon the vice, the oppression, the dishonesty, the mean trickery, and the ugliness of humanity; he brooded over its diseases, and forgot to look sufficiently for healthy symptoms. And this frame of mind to some extent, as far as we can see in the *Vision*, coloured his view of Nature. As a fact he seems to have noticed Nature very little at all, but when he does, except in the opening lines of the poem, she represents to him disaster and the punishment of men, in the form of storms, floods, famine, and pesti-

---

[1] Some passages of the *Vision*, apart from this question, will remind readers of the *Pilgrim's Progress*. The Field of the World recalls Vanity Fair; the description of the Way to Truth, many a phrase concerning the road to the Celestial City; and in each we have a wicket-gate.

lence ; while the character of the allusion to the mist on Malvern Hills may indicate that he had been struck by that immeasurable and illimitable element in Nature, which mocks at the effort of men to control it.

He saw the darker side of life ; of its brighter aspect, of the common good fellowship of men, which appears here and there in every society, in spite of all selfishness ; of the victory of men over wrong ; of the beauty and benignity of the Nature around them, he saw next to nothing. He has a faith that somehow the good will conquer evil, but it is a wavering one, and he sees no clear or practical means to that end.

We may suggest some reasons for this. His melancholic temperament and his poverty, together with his apparent failure to rise in the world, no doubt caused his view of life to be " sicklied o'er with the pale cast of thought " : and the troubles, both mental and physical, which beset the path of the poor man, do not tend to make his vision true and sane ; more especially if, as with Langland, the saving grace of humour has been only scantily allowed to him. Chaucer was at one time in material distress, but his Complaint to his Purse, his " lady dere," witnesses how much humour helped him in the strait.

But a greater reason for Langland's excessively dark view of life lies probably in the fact that he stood apart, as far as we know, from the most hopeful movement of the time against some of the very evils he so bitterly denounced—that earnest and practical movement for social and personal freedom headed by John Ball [1] and other brave spirits, and which was represented in the world of theology by Wyclif. Had he been able to put himself, even in thought, into sympathy with this movement, his eyes would have turned more often than they do, from the diseases of society to its healthy aspirations and its gallant struggle to fulfil them.

As it is, his hope turns, where indeed the hope of every lover of the race finally rests, to the growth of moral goodness in humanity ; but even his trust in that is scarcely firm, and hence comes his wavering faith in the future regeneration of the world. Had he felt a stronger impulse from the progressive movement of his time, in politics, in social life, and in theology, he would, I repeat, have despaired less. His intellectual position, however, with regard to these things was below the high-water mark of humanity in the fourteenth century. He only reached that in his moral and religious ideal ; though there are signs in him that his views on theology were more advanced than those he held concerning politics and social life. With the framework of the political government, and with the plan upon which his society was

---

[1] If readers wish to realise the noblest spirit of that movement and its ideal aim, they cannot do better than turn to William Morris's "Dream of John Ball." The writer has there given a picture of the progressive movement of the fourteenth century in its highest form.

organised, Langland, as I have said before, was apparently content. Work these out faithfully, he thought, and things will go well. Therefore he turns with all his might to insist upon *Do well*— the good and loving life—as the one thing needful for salvation in this world and the world to come. In his high moral ideal he is abreast of the noblest of his age ; " Be true, be honest, be chaste, deal righteously with every man," he says, " but "—and here he passes on to higher ground than that of mere morality—" except ye love faithfully, and give your wealth to the needy, your goodness is as useless as a lamp without a light. Love is the balm of heaven, and no sin can be found in him who useth that remedy."

In this ideal there are few to-day who will not be at one with him. The great moral and spiritual truth he insisted upon is a central one for the true progress of humanity. For, with all the political and social change which modern reformers desire to see accomplished, it will be always needful—in order that their righteous work may not become void, but produce a permanent effect upon the world's true life—to uphold that ideal which, in spite of all his personal gloom, and in the midst of the far darker trouble of the world around him, Langland maintained with a noble tenacity. It is on this account that we have the right to place him gratefully among the true helpers of the world's progress to its consummation.

CHRONOLOGICAL TABLE

OF IMPORTANT EVENTS IN THE TIME OF LANGLAND, TO SOME
OF WHICH HE DIRECTLY REFERS IN *PIERS THE PLOWMAN*.

Adapted, with some changes and additions, from Professor
Skeat's *Piers the Plowman*.

Edward II. deposed [see p. 37] ....*Jan.* 20, 1327
Edward III. begins to reign ....*Jan.* 25, 1327
Edward II. murdered [p. 37] ....*Sept.* 21, 1327
Langland born ....about 1332
Chaucer born 1340
Battle of Creçy..*Aug.* 26, 1346
First great Pestilence ("The Death" or the "Black
    Death ").......................*May* 31, 1348, to *Sept.* 29, 1349
An Ordinance regulating Wages of Labour, &c. [p. 103]... 1349
Statute of Labourers [p. 103] 1351
Treaty of Brétigny [p. 40].............................*May* 8, 1360
Second great Pestilence ....*Aug.* 15, 1361, to *May* 3, 1362
Great storm of wind [p. 57] ....*Saturday, Jan.* 15, 1362
A-Text of *Piers the Plowman* written 1362
Third great Pestilence ....*July* 2 to *Sept.* 29, 1369
A fourth Pestilence ....1375 and 1376
Death of the Black Prince ....*June* 8, 1376
Jubilee of Edward's Accession [? referred to on p. 45] *Feb.*, 1377
Death of Edward III. ....*June* 21, 1377
Speech of John of Gaunt, in his own vindication ...*Oct.* 13, 1377
B-Text of *Piers the Plowman* written 1377
Wycliffe's Translation of the Bible ....about 1380
The Peasant Revolt (known as Wat Tyler's Rebellion) ... 1381
Chaucer writes his "Canterbury Tales" ....about 1387
C-Text of *Piers the Plowman* written ......probably about 1393
Richard II. taken prisoner ....*Aug.* 18, 1399
Poem of *Richard the Redeles* ....*Sept.*, 1399
Richard II. formally deposed...........................*Sept.* 30, 1399
Death of Chaucer 1400
Probable date of death of Langland ....about 1400

PROLOGUE.

The author falls asleep and dreams—His vision of the Field between the Tower and the Dungeon—In the Field are gathered all classes of people, and a king to whom an angel speaks— The rout of rats and mice.

IN a summer season when the sun was warm, I clad me in clothing as a shepherd, in the habit of a hermit of unholy works, and I went far and wide through the world to hear the wonders.

But on a May morning on the Malvern Hills, a marvellous thing befell me ; methought it was of faery.[1] I was outwearied with wandering and went to rest down by a broad bank beside a burn, and as I lay there leaning, and looked in the water, it sounded so merrily that I fell into a slumber.

Then I dreamed a marvellous dream—that I was in a wilderness, I wist not where, and as I looked on high, into the East toward the sun, I beheld upon a hill[2] a tower beautifully wrought. There was a deep dale below,[3] and therein a dungeon

---

[1] *I.e.*, the result of enchantment.
[2] The word *toft* in the original = "a slightly elevated, exposed site."
[3] The *dale* is said to be " westwarde " in the C-text.

with deep and dark ditches, and dreadful to look at. A fair field full of folk I found betwixt the dale and hill, with all manner of men, the mean and the rich, working and wandering as the world requireth. Some put themselves to the plough and full seldom played. They laboured full hard in planting and in sowing, and won what wasters destroy with their gluttony. And some followed pride, and thereafter apparelled themselves and came tricked out in fine clothing.

Many put themselves to prayers and penance ; and all for our Lord's love, hoping to win the bliss of heaven, they lived full straitly ; such as anchorites and hermits, who stay in their cells and covet not to wander through the land seeking dainty living to delight the flesh. And some choose trade, and these prosper the better, for it seemeth to our sight that such men thrive. And some as minstrels are skilled to make mirth and get gold by their glee ; without sin, I grant. But jesters and janglers, the children of Judas, feign fancies and make fools of themselves, and yet have wit at will to work, if they needs must. I will not here prove what Paul preacheth of them, for *Qui turpiloquium loquitur* [1] is Lucifer's servant.

Bidders [2] and beggars moved quickly about with

---

[1] Whoso speaketh filthy speech.

[2] *Bidders* is only a synonym for *beggars*, but I keep the word rather than lose the flavour of the old phrase "bidders and beggeres" which frequently occurs in Langland. To *bid* in Early English is to ask or pray. Compare the old expressions *bidding-prayer*, and to *bid beads*, *i.e.*, to pray prayers.

their bellies and their bags crammed full of bread, and told lying tales for their food and fought in the alehouse. God wot, in gluttony those Robert knaves [1] go to bed, and rise up with ribaldry, and sleep and sorry sloth ever pursue them. Pilgrims and palmers pledged themselves to seek St. James [2] and the saints in Rome. They went on their way with many wise tales, and had leave to lie all their life afterwards. I saw some who said they had sought saints, and in every tale they told it seemed from their speech that their tongues were more tuned to lying than to telling truth. A crowd of hermits with hooked staves went to Walsingham, and their wenches after them ; great and long loobies, who were loath to labour, clothed themselves in copes to be known from the others, and made hermits of themselves to have their ease.

There I found friars of all the four Orders,[3] who preached to the people for their own profit, and interpreted the Gospel as it seemed good to them ; through the greed of their Order [4] they explained it as they would. Many of these master friars may clothe them at their own liking, for their money and their merchandise go together ; for since Charity hath been a chapman, and chief

---

[1] A set of lawless vagabonds, notorious for their outrages when *Piers Plowman* was written. (*Skeat.*)

[2] His shrine was at Compostella, in Galicia.

[3] *I.e.*, the Carmelites, Augustines, Dominicans, and Minorites. ✓

[4] *Lit.* "For covetousness of copes."

confessor of lords,[1] many wonderful things have
happened in a few years. Except Holy Church
and they hold together better, the greatest mischief
on earth will speedily arise.[2]

A Pardoner [3] was preaching there as if he were
a priest ; he brought forth a bull with the bishop's
seals, and said that he himself could absolve them
all of falseness in fasting and of broken vows.
Laymen believed him, and liked his words, and
they came up kneeling to kiss his bulls. He thrust
his brevet in their faces and bleared their eyes,
and gained rings and brooches by his charter.
Thus they give their gold to keep gluttons, and
put their faith in such worthless fellows, who
follow lechery. If the bishop were holy and
worth his two ears, his seal would never be sent
to deceive the people thus. But it is not against
the bishop that the youth preacheth,[4] for the
parish priest and he divide the silver which the
poor folk of the parish ought to have, but for them.

Parsons and parish priests complained to the

[1] This alludes to the money received by friars for hearing confessions ; and the friars literally resembled pedlars when they
carried about with them knives and pins to give away to women.
See the *Friar* in Chaucer's Prologue. (*Skeat.*)

[2] The regular friars and secular clergy quarrelled fiercely as to
the right of hearing confessions.

[3] A seller of pardons.

[4] Professor Skeat considers this passage to be "slightly
humorous," meaning, "but you may be sure that it is never
against (or with reference to the bishop) that he preaches." For
the Pardoner had obtained leave to preach and give pardons
from the bishop himself.

bishop that their parishes had been poor since the time of the pestilence,[1] that they might get license and leave to dwell in London and sing for simony the service there ; for silver is sweet.

Bishops and novices, both masters and doctors, who hold their cures under Christ, and have the tonsure in token and sign that they should shrive their parishioners and preach and pray for them and feed the poor, live in London in Lent and at other times. Some serve the King and count out his silver ; they claim his debts in Exchequer and Chancery from the Wards[2] and Wardmotes,[3] and also claim waifs and strays.[4] And some as servants serve lords and ladies, and sit as stewards giving judgment ;[5] their Mass and Matins and many of their Hours[6] are done undevoutly. It is to be feared that Christ at the last will curse full many of them in His Court.[7]

As to the power to bind and to unbind, that Peter had in charge, as the Book telleth, I perceived how he left it with love, as our Lord

---

[1] Between 1348 and 1376 there were several great pestilences. Probably the first, that of 1348, is here meant.

[2] Divisions of the city.

[3] The courts or meetings held in the *Wards*.

[4] Property without an owner and strayed cattle (*Wright*); but the old sense of *stray* also meant goods which a stranger leaves behind him at death, and which go to the king or lord for default of heirs. (*Skeat.*)

[5] They took secular occupation for sake of gain.

[6] Canonical hours, prayers made at stated times in the day.

[7] Lit., "in the Consistory," *i.e.*, the Church council, or assembly of prelates; here used of the Day of Judgment.

bade, amongst four virtues,[1] the best of all the virtues, which are called Cardinals, and Closing Gates,[2] where Christ reigneth in His kingdom, to close and to shut and to open it unto them, and to show Heaven's bliss. But as concerning the cardinals at court[3] who received that name, and presumed they had power in themselves to make a pope ; that they have that power that Peter had I will not call in question ; for the election belongeth to love and to learning, therefore I can, and cannot, speak more of that court.[4]

Then there came a King, led by Knighthood, and the power of the Commons made him reign. And then came Mother-wit and made clerks[5] to counsel the King and to care for the commonweal.

The King and Knighthood and Clergy planned that the Commons should provide for themselves.[6] The Commons then devised handicrafts which Mother-wit could undertake, and ploughmen[7] were

---

[1] *I.e.*, St. Peter deputed the power of the keys to the four cardinal virtues,—Prudence, Temperance, Fortitude, and Justice.

[2] This is a sort of translation of the Lat. *cardinalis*, derived from *cardo*, a hinge. The power of the keys is, as it were, made for the moment, into a power of the hinges. (*Skeat.*)

[3] *I.e.*, at the court of Rome.

[4] I *can* speak more, for I have much I could say about them : yet I *cannot* speak more, out of reverence, for the power of electing a pope is a high and holy thing. (*Skeat.*)

[5] Students and men of learning.

[6] *Themselves* appears to stand here for *all of them ;* the C-text reads "*provide their provisions.*"

[7] These seem to be counted as a fifth class, and looked upon as inferior to the rest.

ordained for the profit of all the people, to till and to labour, as honest life requireth.

The King and the Commons and Mother-wit, the third, made Law and Loyalty, that each man might know his own. Then a lunatic looked up, a lean thing[1] withal, and kneeling said, scholar-wise, to the King: "Christ keep thee, Sir King, and also thy kingdom, and grant thee so to govern thy land that Loyalty may love thee, and thou be rewarded in Heaven for thy righteous rule."

And then, in the air on high, an angel of Heaven stooped to speak in Latin—so that laymen might not discuss nor judge what should justify them, but suffer and serve—therefore the angel said :—

"Sum Rex, sum Princeps · neutrum fortasse deinceps ;—
O qui iura regis · Christi specialia regis,
Hoc quod agas melius · iustus es, esto pius !
Nudum ius a te · vestiri vult pietate ;
Qualia vis metere · talia grana sere.
Si ius nudatur · nudo de iure metatur ;
Si seritur pietas · de pietate metas !"[2]

---

[1] The word *thing* merely signifies here a *creature* or *person*, there is no contempt in the use of it.

[2] (You say) "I am a king, I am a prince," (but you will be) "neither perhaps hereafter.
O thou who dost administer the special laws of Christ the King, [merciful !
That thou mayst do this the better, as thou art just, be Naked justice requires to be clothed by thee with mercy, Whatever crops thou wouldst reap, such be sure to sow.
If justice is stripped bare, let bare justice be reaped by thee ;
If mercy is sown, mayst thou reap of mercy !"
(*Adapted from Skeat's translation.*)

Then a glutton of words, a Goliardus,[1] was angry
and answered afterwards to the angel on high :—

> " Dum rex a regere · dicatur nomen habere,
> Nomen habet sine re · nisi studet iura tenere." [2]

And then all the Commons cried in Latin verse,
for the King's counsel—if any would interpret—
" *Precepta Regis sunt nobis vincula legis.*" [3]

With that there ran all at once a rout of rats [4]
and small mice, more than a thousand, with them,
and came to a council for their common profit.
For a Cat of a Court came when he liked and
caught them easily, and seized them whenever he
would, and played with them perilously, and pushed
them about. " For fear of divers dangers we dare
not look about us ; and if we grumble at his game

---

[1] A word which went through many changes of meaning. It
comes originally from the word *Golias*, a term invented by
Walter Map (a satirist of the 13th century). "He named his
imaginary bishop Golias, after the Philistine slain by David ;
not without some reference, perhaps, to the O. French *goule*,
Lat. *gula*, gluttony. Soon after *Goliardus* meant a clerical
buffoon ; later still it meant any *jougleur*, or teller of ribald
stories ; in which sense it is used by Chaucer." (*Skeat.*) It here
stands for " a glutton of words," one who was full of long pieces
which he could recite.

[2] While a ruler is said to have his name (from ruling),
He has the name without the thing unless he study to keep
the laws.

[3] The precepts of the king are for us the bonds of law.

[4] In this version of the ancient fable the rats are the citizens
and influential commoners; the mice are the less important folk;
the cat is Edward III., or, as some say, John of Gaunt, and the
kitten is his grandson Richard, then heir to the throne, and
afterwards Richard II.

he will vex us all, scratch us, or claw us, or hold
us in his clutches, so that we loathe our life before
he letteth go of us. If we could by any device
withstand his will, we might lord it up above, out
of his reach, and live at our ease."

A rat of renown, very ready of tongue, said that
to his mind this was the sovereign remedy : " I
have seen men," he said, " in the city of London,
bearing bright rings about their necks, and some
with collars of cunning workmanship ; they run
loose both in warren and waste wherever they
please, and at other times they go elsewhere, as I
hear tell. Were there a bell on their collar, by
Jesu, methinketh men might know where they
were going and run away. And right so," said
that rat, " reason telleth me to buy a bell of brass
or of bright silver, and fasten it on to a collar
for our common good, and hang it upon the Cat's
neck, and then we can hear whether he moveth
or resteth or runneth to play ; and if he like to
play then we can know it, and appear in his
presence as long as it pleaseth him to sport ; and
if he grow wrathful, beware and shun his path."

All the rout of rats agreed to this plan, but
when the bell was bought and hanged upon the
collar there was no rat in all the company who
durst, for the realm of France, have bound the bell
about the Cat's neck, nor have hung it about the
Cat's throat to win all England. And they held
themselves not bold enough and their counsel

4

weak, and they held their labour lost and all their long devising.

A mouse, who had good parts, methought, struck forth sternly to the front and stood before them all, and to the rout of rats spake these words : " Though we killed the Cat yet would there come another to scratch us and all our kind, though we should creep under benches. Therefore I counsel all the commons to let the Cat be, and never be so foolhardy as to show him the bell. For I heard my sire say, seven years ago, that where the Cat is a Kitten the court is full wretched. Holy Writ witnesseth to that, if one will read it : *Ve terre vbi puer rex est,* etc.[1] For no man may have rest there by night for the rats ; while he[2] catcheth rabbits our carrion he coveteth not, but feedeth himself with naught but venison—may we never defame him ! For better is a little loss than a long sorrow —confusion amongst us all, if the Cat died, though we got rid of a tyrant. For we mice would destroy many men's malt, and also ye rout of rats would rend men's clothes were there not that Cat of the Court who can catch you ; and had ye rats your will ye would not rule yourselves. As for me," said the mouse, " I see so much that would come afterwards that never shall the Cat or the Kitten be vexed by my counsel. And talk no more of this collar, that never cost me aught, and though it had cost my goods I would not confess it, but

[1] Woe to thee, O land, whose king is a boy.   [2] *I.e.,* the Cat.

suffer him to do as he pleaseth, fastened and un-
fastened, to catch what he may. Therefore every
wise man I warn : let him look well to his own."

What this dream meaneth, ye merry men, divine
ye ; for, by dear God in Heaven, I dare not.

Also in that field there moved about a hundred
in silken coifs, they seemed like serjeants at the
Bar. They pleaded the law for pence and pounds,
and would not once unloose their lips for simple
love of our Lord. Sooner mightest thou measure
the mist on Malvern Hills than get a mumble from
their mouth, except money were shown them.

Barons and burgesses and bondmen also I saw
in this assembly, as ye shall afterwards hear.
Bakers and brewers and many butchers, wool-
weavers and weavers of linen, tailors and tinkers
and collectors of dues in the markets, masons and
miners, and many other crafts. There moved
about every kind of labourer living, such as ditchers
and delvers who do their work ill and spend the
long day in "*Dieu vous save Dame Emma.*" [1]

Cooks and their knaves cried, "Hot pies, hot !
Good pigs and geese ! Come and dine, come and
dine !" Taverners, too, called "White wine of
Alsace, and red wine of Gascony, wine of the
Rhine and wine of Rochelle, to wash down the
roast !"

All this I saw asleep, and seven times more.

---

[1] "God save you, Dame Emma," the refrain of a popular
song.

PASSUS I.

A lovely lady tells him the meaning of the Tower and Dungeon —She is Holy Church, and instructs him concerning Truth, Pride, and Love.

WHAT this mountain meaneth, and the dark dale and the field full of folk, I will show you plainly.

A lady of lovely countenance and clothed in linen came down from a castle and called to me graciously and said, " Son,[1] sleepest thou ? Seest thou the people, how busy in the crowd they are ? Most of these people who live on earth, if they have honour in the world wish for nothing better ; of any other heaven than here they hold no reckoning."

Though she was fair I was afraid of her face, and said, " Pardon, madam, what meaneth this ? "

" In the tower on the hill," she said, " is Truth ; and He would that ye should do as His word teacheth you, for He is the Father of Faith who made you all, both fell [2] and face, and gave you

---

[1] The C-text has " Will "—a proper name, and Langland's own.

[2] *I.e.*, skin. I have kept the original word for the sake of alliteration ; it is still in use for the skin of an animal, a hide.

five wits to honour Him therewith, while ye are here. And therefore He bade the earth provide each of you at your need with wool and with linen and with food, in such measure as to give you ease. And graciously commanded three things in common ; none but those are needful, and I will name them and reckon them up rightly, and afterwards do thou repeat them :—The one is clothing to keep thee from the cold, and then meat for meals to keep off discomfort, and drink when thou art dry. But do nothing out of measure, lest thou be the worse when thou shouldst work. Therefore dread delicious drink and thou shalt do the better ; moderation is a medicine, though thou mayst yearn for much. Not all that the body asketh is good for the spirit, nor is all life to thy body that is dear to thy soul. Believe not thy body, for a liar teacheth it, to wit, the wretched world which would betray thee. For the devil and the flesh together follow thee, both this and that pursue thy soul and whisper in thine heart ; and that thou mayest be wary I teach thee the best."

" Pardon, madam," I said, " your words please me well, but the money of the earth that men hold so fast, tell me, madam, to whom that treasure belongeth ? "

"Go to the gospel," said she, "that God Himself spoke when the people questioned Him in the temple about a penny, whether they should therewith honour Cæsar the king. And God asked of them, Of whom spake the superscription and likewise the image that stood thereon ? '*Cesaris,*' they said, 'we all see him plainly.' '*Reddite Cesari,*'[1] said God, 'what *Cesari* belongeth, *et que sunt dei, deo,*[2] or else ye do ill.' For rightful Reason should rule you all, and Mother-wit be warden to keep your wealth, and be guardian of your treasure and at need deliver it to you, for those two and Thriftiness hold together."

Then I asked her plainly, by Him who made her, " I beseech you, madam, what may mean that dungeon in the dale, that is dreadful to look at ? "

" That is the Castle of Care, and whoso cometh therein may curse that he was born either body or soul. A man dwelleth therein who is called Wrong, the Father of Falsehood, and he built it. He egged on Adam and Eve to do ill, and he counselled Cain to kill his brother, and beguiled Judas with the Jews' silver, and then hanged him afterwards on an elder tree. He is the hinderer of Love and lieth to every one, and those who trust in his treasure he betrayeth the soonest."

Then I wondered in my mind what woman it might be who taught such wise words from Holy Writ, and in the High Name I asked her, ere she went away, who verily she was who counselled me so graciously.

[1] Render to Cæsar.
[2] And [the things] which are of God to God.

" I am Holy Church," she said, " thou oughtest
know me ; I received thee the first and taught
thee the faith, and thou didst bring me sureties
that thou wouldst fulfil my bidding and love me
faithfully while thy life shalt endure."

Then I fell on my knees and besought mercy of
her, and begged her piteously to pray for my sins,
and also to teach me kindly to believe on Christ,
so that I might do His will who made me man.
" Show me the way to no treasure, but tell me
this one thing—how I may save my soul, O thou
who art accounted holy ! "

" When all treasures have been tried," she said,
" Truth is the best. I call to witness the text
Deus caritas[1] to prove it. It is as precious a
treasure as dear God Himself. Whosoever is true
of tongue and telleth truth alone, and doth works
accordingly and wisheth no man ill, on earth and
above he is a god, the gospel saith, and like our
Lord, according to St. Luke's words. The clerks
who know this should teach it over the land, for
Christian and unchristian claim alike to learn the
truth. Kings and knights should keep it rightly,
and ride and speed through the kingdoms, and
take *transgressores* and bind them fast, till Truth
had determined their trespass. And that is plainly
the profession for knights, and not to fast upon
one Friday in five score winters, but rather to hold
with him and with her who would do the truth

[1] God is love.

wholly, and never leave them for love or receiving of silver. For David in his day dubbed knights, and made them swear on their sword for ever to serve Truth; and whosoever overstepped that point was *apostata*[1] in the order. But Christ, the King of kings, knighted ten Orders, Cherubin, and Seraphin, and seven more such, and one other, and by His majesty gave them power and made them archangels over His lower servants, and it seemed then the happier to them. And He taught them to know the truth concerning the Trinity, and to be obedient to His bidding; naught else did He command them.

"Lucifer learned this in Heaven with the legions, but because he obeyed not he lost his happiness; and fell from that fellowship in a devil's likeness into a deep and dark hell to dwell there for ever; and more thousands than man could number went forth in loathsome form, for they believed upon him who deceived them in this manner : *Ponam pedem in aquilone, et similis ero altissimo.*[2] And all who hoped it might be so, no heaven could hold them ; but they were falling from it for nine days together, till God in His goodness paused and stayed, and bade the heavens close fast and stand quiet. When these wicked went forth they fell in a wonderful way ; some abode in the air, some

[1] Apostate. "An *apostata* was one who quitted his order *after* he had completed the year of his novitiate."

[2] I will place my foot in the North, and shall be even as the Most High.

on earth, and some deep in hell ; but Lucifer lieth the lowest of them all. His pain shall have no end, because of the pride that he showed ; and all that do wrong they shall go and dwell with that shrew after their death. But as Holy Writ telleth us, those that do well and make their end, as I said before, in truth (that is the best), may be sure that their soul shall go to Heaven, where Truth is, in Trinity, and enthroneth them all. Therefore I say, as before I said, by witness of these texts, When all treasures are tried, Truth is the best. Teach this to these unlearned men (for the learned men know it) — that Truth is the choicest treasure on earth."

"Yet have I no understanding,"[1] I said ; " still must ye teach me further as to Truth ; by what power it commenceth to live in my body, and where it beginneth."

"Thou foolish dolt," she said, "thy wits are dull, thou learnedst too little Latin, man, in thy youth. *Heu michi, quod sterilem duxi vitam iuuenilem!*[2] It is Conscience,[1] verily, that doth teach thee in thy heart to love thy Lord better than thyself, and to do no deadly sin though thou shouldst die for it. This I believe according to Truth ; if any can tell thee better see that thou suffer him to speak, and then teach it afterwards.

---

[1] *Kynde knowing, i.e.,* literally, natural understanding, or *Conscience,* as I have translated it a few lines further on.
[2] Woe is me ! because I have led a barren life in my youth.

"For thus His word witnesseth, and do thou hereafter, for Truth saith that Love is the balm of Heaven, and no sin can be found in him who useth that kind of remedy. All His works He hath wrought with love as it pleased Him, and He taught it to Moses for the worthiest thing and most like to Heaven ; and also it is the plant of peace and the most precious of virtues. For Heaven could not hold it,[1] it was so heavy in itself, till it had eaten its fill of the earth. And when it had of this earth taken flesh and blood, there was never a leaf upon linden lighter ; and it was light and piercing as the point of a needle, so that no armour nor no high walls could hinder it. Therefore Love is the leader of the people of the Lord of Heaven, and a mediator, as the Mayor is between the King and the Commons. Even so is Love a leader and maketh the law, and fineth a man for his misdeeds. And for to know of it naturally, it beginneth through (Divine) power and hath its head and well-spring in the heart.

"For in Conscience (Divine) power springeth in the heart, and that is of the Father who made us all, who looked on us with love and let His Son die meekly for our misdeeds to amend us all. And yet He wished no woe tò them who wrought for Him that suffering, but meekly He besought Mercy

---

[1] *I.e.,* " love ; here used of the love of Christ, which heaven could not contain, till it had ' eaten its fill of the earth ' ; *i.e.,* participated in the human nature by Incarnation." (*Skeat.*)

to have pity on the people who tortured Him to death. Here thou mightest see example in Himself alone : that He was mighty and meek and granted mercy to them who hanged Him on high and pierced His heart. Therefore I counsel you rich, have pity on the poor ; though ye be powerful to bring to justice, be meek in your deeds, for with the same measure that ye mete, evil or otherwise, ye shall be weighed therewith when ye go hence. *Eadem mensura qua mensi fueritis, remecietur vobis.*[1] And though ye be true of tongue and earn honestly your livelihood, and be as chaste as a child who weepeth in church,[2] yet except ye love faithfully and give to the poor, and distribute well such wealth as God hath sent you, ye shall have no more merit in Mass nor in Hours than Malkyn [3] hath of her maidenhood that no man desireth. For James the Gentle in his books hath laid it down that faith without the deed is verily nothing worth, and as dead.as a door-post unless deeds follow it. *Fides sine operibus mortua est*, etc.[4]

" Therefore Chastity without Charity shall be chained in hell ; it is as useless as a lamp that hath no light. Many chaplains are chaste, but have no charity ; and no men are more covetous than they

---

[1] With the same measure which ye shall have measured, it shall be measured to you again.

[2] Probably refers to a child being baptized.

[3] A proverbial name for an unchaste slattern. (*Skeat.*)

[4] Faith without works is dead, &c.

when they are advanced. They are unkind to their kindred and to all Christians ; they devour what they should give in charity and cry for more. Such chastity without charity shall be chained in hell ! Many ' curatoures '[1] keep them clean of body, but they are cumbered with covetousness and cannot put it from them, for avarice hath so hardly bound them up together. And that is no truth of the Trinity, but treachery of hell, and a lesson to laymen to give alms all the later.[2] Therefore these words are written in the gospel : *Date et dabitur vobis*,[3] for I give to all of you. And that is the lock of love and letteth out my grace, that it may comfort the troubled who are cumbered with sin.

" Love is the leech[4] of life, and nearest our Lord Himself, and also the straight road that leadeth into Heaven ; and therefore I say, as I said before, according to the texts, when all treasures are tried Truth is the best.

" Now I have told you what Truth is—that no treasure is better—no longer may I tarry with thee. Now our Lord keep thee ! "

[1] *I.e.*, guardians of heirs under age.
[2] *I.e.*, to put off giving alms altogether.
[3] Give and it shall be given to you.
[4] *I.e.*, physician.

PASSUS II.

Holy Church tells the dreamer of Meed and Falsehood and their proposed marriage—The wedding is arranged, but Theology objects—All the company ride to London to try the case at Westminster—They reach the King's Court, and he vows to punish them; they all run away, except the Lady Meed.

YET still I knelt and prayed favour from her, and said : " Pardon, Madam, for the love of Mary of Heaven, who bare that blessed Child that bought us on the Rood, teach me by some means to know Falsehood."

" Look upon thy left hand and lo, where he standeth ! both Falsehood and Flattery and their many fellows ! "

I looked on my left hand, as the lady told me, and was aware of a woman clothed beautifully, having a robe bordered with fur the finest on earth ; and she was crowned with a crown, the king hath no better. Her fingers were daintily adorned with gold wire, and red rubies were thereon, as red as any gleed,¹ and diamonds of

¹ *I.e.*, burning coal or spark of fire.

21

greatest worth and twofold manner of sapphires, orientals[1] and beryls, to destroy venom.[2]   Her robe was exceeding rich, dyed with red scarlet, with bands of red gold and precious stones.   Her array ravished me, such riches I had never seen, and I wondered what woman she was, and whose wife she might be.

"What is this woman," I said, "so richly attired ? "

"That is Meed the Maid," [3] she answered, "who hath full often vexed me, and hath spoken ill of my lover who is called Loyalty.[4]   And she hath belied him to the lords who guard the laws.   She is as familiar as myself in the Pope's palace ; but Soothness would not have it so, for she is a bastard, and Flattery was her father, who hath a deceitful tongue, and hath never told the truth since he came upon earth.   And the ways of Meed

---

[1] Langland's word here is *orientales*—to be distinguished from the preceding word *safferes*.   "The precious stones called by the lapidaries *Oriental Ruby*, *Oriental Topaz*, *Oriental Amethyst*, and *Oriental Emerald*, are red, yellow, violet, and green sapphires, distinguishable from the other gems of the same name, which have not the prefix *Oriental* by their greatly superior hardness, and greater specific gravity" (quoted from *Eng. Cyclop.* by Prof. Skeat.)

[2] "It was a common belief that precious stones would cure diseases, and that they were as antidotes against poison" (*Skeat*).

[3] The Lady *Meed* represents both *Reward in general* and *Bribery in particular ;* her name is sometimes used in one sense only ; sometimes with a mingling of both meanings.   See Passus IV. for an explanation of the two kinds of Meed.

[4] Or Good-faith.

are as his, right as kinship must needs have it. *Qualis pater, talis filius ; bona arbor bonum fructum facit.*[1] I ought to be higher than she, for I came of a better line. My father is the great God and the ground of every grace, one God without beginning, and I am His true daughter ; and He hath given me Mercy in marriage, and whatsoever man be merciful and love me faithfully, he shall be my lord and I his beloved in the high Heaven. And whatsoever man taketh Meed, I dare lay my head that for her love he shall lose a share of *Caritas.*[2] How speaketh David the King concerning the men who receive Meed, and the men who uphold Truth ? And the Psalter beareth witness how ye shall save yourselves : *Domine, quis habitabit in tabernaculo tuo ?* &c.[3]

"And now this Meed is to be married withal to, a cursed shrew, to one Falsehood-Fickle[4]-tongue, who was begotten of a devil. Flattery, through his fair speech, hath bewitched this people, and it is wholly Liar's doing that Meed is thus to be wedded. To-morrow is to be the maiden's bridal, and there thou mayest see, if thou wilt, who they all are, both the less and the greater, who follow with them. Learn to know them all there, if thou canst, and keep thy tongue, and speak not against

---

[1] As the father so the son ; a good tree bears good fruit.
[2] Charity.
[3] Lord, who shall dwell in Thy tabernacle ? &c.
[4] *Fikel*, in Middle English, does not mean *changeable*, but *treacherous.*

them, but let them be, till Loyalty be Justice and have power to punish them ; then put forth thy reason.[1] Now I commit thee to Christ and to His pure mother," she said, " and let Conscience never trouble thee because of Meed's avarice."

Thus that lady left me lying asleep.

And in a dream methought I saw how Meed was married. All the rich retinue that bear rule with Falsehood, on each side, were bidden to the bridal ; all kinds of men both mean and rich. Many a man was assembled to marry this maiden, such as knights and clerks, and also common people ; sizers[2] and summoners,[3] sheriffs and their clerks, beadles and bailiffs, and brokers of mer- chandise, forerunners[4] and victuallers, and advo- cates of the Court of Arches. I cannot reckon the rout that ran about Meed.

But Simony and Civil[5] and sizers of Courts were most familiar with Meed, methought, of any men ; but Flattery was the first to fetch her from her bower, and like a broker,[6] brought her to be joined

[1] This probably means " Then make thy complaint against them."

[2] A *sisour* was (1) a person deputed to hold assizes ; and (2) a juror, though not quite in the modern sense. (*Skeat.*)

[3] A *summoner*. An officer who summons delinquents to appear in an ecclesiastical court ; now called an *apparitor*. (*Skeat.*)

[4] The original word is *forgoeres :* " People whose business it was to go before the great lords in their progresses, and buy up provisions for them " (*Wright*, quoted by Prof. Skeat).

[5] Civil = the Civil Law.

[6] *Broker* is here used in the general sense of a contriver of bargains, a matchmaker. (*Skeat.*)

to Falsehood, and when Simony and Civil saw that this was the will of both they agreed, for silver, to ⌐ say according as they wished. Then Liar came forth and said, " Lo, here ! A charter that Guile with his great oaths hath given them both ! " and he prayed Civil to look and Simony to read it. Then Simony and Civil both stand forth and unfold the deed of gift that Falsehood hath made, and thus these men proclaim with a loud voice :

" *Sciant presentes et futuri*, &c.[1] Know and witness, ye that dwell upon this earth, that Meed is married more for her goods than for any virtue or beauty, or any noble birth. Falseness is glad of her for he knoweth her to be rich, and Flattery with his guileful speech granteth them, by this charter, to be princes in pride and to despise poverty, to backbite and to boast and to bear false witness, to scorn and to scold and to` make slander, and, bold and disobedient, to break the ten commandments. And the Earldom of Envy and Wrath together ; with the little castle of Strife and chattering-out-of-reason ; the County of Covetousness ; and all the country round, that is, Usury and Avarice, I give them altogether, in bargains and in treaties, with the whole borough of Theft ; and all the length and breadth of the lordship of Lechery, such as deeds and words and glancing of eyes, raiment and wishings, and idle

[1] Be it known unto all men, &c.

5

thoughts where the will desired and the doing faileth." Gluttony he gave them also, together with great oaths, and to drink all day at divers taverns, and there to gossip and gibe and judge their fellow-Christians, and on fasting-days to eat before the full time, and then to sit and sup till sleep assail them, and breed as town-swine, and lie in bed easily, till sloth and sleep make them [1] sleek ; and then shall Despair [2] awaken them without the will to amend, for they believe they are lost ; this is their last end.

And he gave them to have and to hold and their heirs after them, a dwelling with the devil and be damned for ever, with all the pains of Purgatory and the torment of Hell ; paying their souls to Satan for this thing at one year's end, to suffer torments with him, and to dwell with him in woe while God is in Heaven.

In witness of which thing Wrong was the first, and Piers the Pardoner of the Pauline Order,[3] Bat the beadle of Buckinghamshire, Rainald the reeve of the Soke of Rutland,[4] Munde the Miller, and many others more. "In the date of the Devil

---

[1] There is an abrupt change here in the pronouns, from the plural to the singular, which, for the sake of clearness, I have left unexpressed in the translation.

[2] *Wanhope* is the fine original word, *i.e. unhope.*

[3] An order of monks or friars, perhaps to be identified with the "Crutched Friars."

[4] The term *soken* or *soke* is a law term, meaning (1) a privilege, (2) (as here) the district within which such a privilege or power is exercised. (*Skeat.*)

I seal this deed, by the witness of Sir Simony and by leave of Civil."

Then Theology was vexed when he heard this tale, and said to Civil, "Now mayest thou have sorrow for making such weddings to anger Truth ; and ere this wedding be made, Woe betide thee ! For Meed is a woman begotten of Amends, and God agreeth to give Meed to Truth and thou hast given her to a deceiver. Now God give thee sorrow ! For *dignus est operarius* [1] to have his hire, and thou hast joined her to Falsehood. Fie on thy law ! For thou livest wholly by lies and by unclean works. Simony and thyself are a shame to Holy Church, and the notaries and ye vex the people; ye shall pay for it both, by God that made me ! Full well know ye, liars, except your wits fail you, that Falsehood is faithless and treacherous in his ways, and was a bastard born of Beelzebub's kin. And Meed is a lady, and a wealthy maiden, and might kiss the King for cousin, an she would. Therefore do now according both to wisdom and wit, and take her to London, where the law is declared, and see if any law will let them join together ; and though Justices may declare her to be joined with Falsehood, yet beware of wedding them, for Truth is wise, and Conscience is of his counsel and knoweth each one of you ; and if he find you faulty and holding with the false, full bitterly shall it beset your souls at the last."

[1] Worthy is the labourer.

Civil assenteth hereto, but Simony would not until he had silver for his service, as well as the notaries. Then Flattery brought forth florins enough, and bade Guile give gold all about and especially to the notaries that none might fail them, and to fee False-witness with florins enough, " That he may manage Meed and bring about my will."

When this gold was given, great were the thanks to Falsehood and to Flattery for their fair gifts, and they came to comfort Falsehood against anxiety, and said, " Verily, sir, we shall never cease till Meed through all our wits be thy wedded wife. For we have managed Meed with our pleasant speech so that she agreeth with a good will to go to London, to see if the law will allow you to be together in joy for ever."

Then was Falseness glad and Flattery also pleased, and caused all men in the shires round about to be summoned, and bade them all be ready, beggars and others, to go with them to Westminster to witness this matter. But then were they in a strait for horses to take them thither, and Flattery fetched forth many foals, and set Meed upon a sheriff all newly shod, and Falsehood sat on a sizer who trotted gently, and Flattery on a flatterer finely attired. But when the notaries had no horses they were vexed, because Simony and Civil must go on foot. And then Simony and Civil both swore that summoners should be saddled and serve for each of them, and they bade apparel the provisors [1] like palfreys. "Sir Simony himself shall sit upon their back. Bring together deans and subdeans ; and let them saddle archdeacons and officials and all your registrars with silver (that they may allow our sins, such as adultery, divorce, and secret usury), and let them carry bishops about on their visitations. The trusty friends of the Paulines, as concerning complaints in the Consistory, shall serve me who am called Civil ; and harness the commissary [2] and he shall draw our cart, and provide us victuals from *fornicatores.* And make of Liar a long cart to take all these others, such as friars and vagabonds who run on foot."

And thus went forth Falsehood and Flattery together, and Meed between them, and all these men after. I cannot stay to tell of the train of all manner of men that follow them, but Guile was their outrider and led them all.

Soothness saw them full well and said but little, and spurred his palfrey and passed them all ; he came to the King's Court and told it to Conscience,

---

[1] *Provisor* is used here in the sense of one that sued to the Court of Rome for a *provision.* A *provision* meant the providing of a bishop or any other person with an ecclesiastical living by the Pope, before the death of the actual incumbent. (*Skeat.*)

[2] "An officer of the bishop, who exercises spiritual jurisdiction in places of the diocese so far distant from the episcopal see, that the chancellor cannot call the people to the bishop's consistory court, without putting them to inconvenience" (*Imp. Dict.,* quoted by Professor Skeat).

and Conscience afterwards told it again to the King.

"Now, by Christ," said the King, "if I could catch Falsehood or Flattery, or any of his fellows, I would be avenged on those wretches that do so ill, and let hang them by the neck, and all that abet them. No man on earth shall go bail for the least of them, but right as the law will find, so let it fall on them all."

And he commanded a constable to come straightway, and "Arrest those oppressors at any cost, I bid you ; and fetter Falseness fast, in spite of any gifts, and cut off Guile's head, and let him go no further. And if ye catch Liar, let him not escape for any prayer, I command you, till he be put in the pillory ; and bring Meed to me in spite of them all."

Dread stood at the door and heard the judgment, and how the King commanded constables and servants to fetter and bind Falseness and his company. Then Dread went quickly and warned Falsehood, and bade him and all his fellows flee for fear. Falseness for fear then fled to the friars ; and Guile was almost affrighted to death, but merchants met with him and made him stay with them, and shut him up in their shops to show their wares, and apparelled him as a prentice to serve the people.

Then Liar ran quickly away, and lurked in the lanes, and was pulled hither and thither by many a one. Because of his many lies he was nowhere welcome, but everywhere he was hooted at and bidden pack off, until the pardoners had pity on him and pulled him indoors. They washed him and wiped him, and clothed him in old raiment, and sent him with seals to churches on Sunday, and he gave pardons for pence everywhere, by pounds at a time. Then the leeches began to lour, and sent letters for Liar to dwell with them to inspect waters. Sellers of spices spoke with him to look at their wares, for he understood their trade and knew many spices. But minstrels and messengers once met him, and kept him half a year and eleven days ; and then friars with fair speech brought him thence, and clothed him as a friar, that strangers might not know him ; but he hath leave to go out as oft as pleaseth him, and when he will stay is welcome, and he dwelleth often with them.[1]

All fled away for fear and escaped into corners, save Meed the Maid none others durst abide. But to tell truly, she was trembling for fear, and she wept also and wrung her hands when she was taken.

[1] The C-text adds : "Simony and Civil sent to Rome, and by appeals put themselves in the Pope's favour. But Conscience accused them both to the King, and said : 'By Christ, Sir King, except these clerks amend, thy kingdom will grow evil through their avarice, and Holy Church through them be injured for ever.' "

PASSUS III.

Meed is brought to the King's presence, who bids that she be well lodged—The Justices and others visit her—She is shriven—The King proposes that she shall marry Conscience—Conscience refuses, and exposes her—She retaliates and Conscience refutes her.

Now with beadles and bailiffs Meed the Maid, and none other of them all, is brought before the King. And the King called a clerk, whose name I know not, to take Meed the Maid and lodge her in comfort.

"I will try her myself, and truly question her, What man on earth might be dearest to her ; and if she do after my counsel and follow my will, I will forgive her this guilt, so God help me."

Then the clerk did as the king bade, and took Meed courteously by the waist and brought her to a chamber, and there was mirth and minstrelsy to please Meed. They that dwell in Westminster all honoured her ; and some of the Justices, by the leave of Learning, went gladly and graciously to the chamber where the lady dwelled, that they might comfort her kindly, and said :

"Mourn not, Meed, nor be sorrowful, for we will

32

counsel the King, and make way for thee that thou
mayest be wedded at thy will and where it pleaseth
thee, notwithstanding all device or craft of Conscience, as I trow ! "

Then Meed thanked them all humbly for their
great goodness, and gave to each of them goblets of
pure gold, and cups of silver, and rings with rubies,
and many other rich things ; and she gave the least
man of their train a coin [1] of gold ; and then these
lords took their leave of Meed.

With that there came clerks likewise to comfort
her ; and they bade her be blithe, " For we are
thine own to do thy will while thou livest." Then,
graciously she promised them also to " Love you
faithfully and to make you lords, and in the Consistory at the Court to get your names called, and
no ignorance shall hinder the man that I love,
that he be not advanced to the first place, for I
am acknowledged where clever clerks shall lag
behind ! "

Then there came a confessor clothed as a friar,
to Meed the Maid he spoke these words, and said
full softly, as it were in confession : " Though men
learned and unlearned had both lain by thee, and
though Falseness had followed thee all these fifty
winters, I will absolve thee myself for a horse-
load of wheat, and be also thy beadsman,[2] and

---

[1] Lit. a *motoun* of gold, so called from its bearing the impres-
sion of a *lamb* or *mutton* upon one side of it. (*Skeat.*)

[2] One who prays for another for money.

bear well thy message to knights and clerks that
Conscience may be turned."

Then for her misdeeds Meed kneeled to that
man, and I trow she shrived her shamelessly of
her wickedness, and told him a lying tale, and
gave him a noble that he might be her beadsman
and her broker also.　Then he soon absolved her,
and said afterwards :

" We have a window a-making which will cost
us full much, wouldst thou glaze that gable[1] and
grave thy name therein, thy soul would be sure to
enter heaven."

" If I knew that," said the woman, " I would not
spare to be your friend, friar, and never fail you,
while ye have lords that follow lechery, and lack
not ladies who love well the same.　It is frailty of
flesh, ye may find it in books, and a habit of nature
whereof we all come ;　whoso may escape the
slander, the harm is soon amended.　It is the sin
of the seven soonest forgiven.　Have mercy,"
said Meed, " on men that follow it, and I will roof
your church and build your cloisters, whiten your
walls and glaze your windows, and paint and
pourtray and pay for the work, so every　one
shall say I am a sister[2] of your house."

But[3] God forbiddeth all good people such

[1] Gable-end of a church.

[2] The word *sister* has a direct allusion to the letters of
fraternity, by means of which any wealthy person could belong
to a religious order of the mendicant friars.　(*Skeat.*)

[3] This passage is of course the author's own reflection on the
above transaction.

engraving, that they should write their good deeds in windows, lest pride and pomp of the world be painted there. For Christ knoweth thy conscience and thine inmost will, and thy spending and thy covetousness, and who really owned the wealth. Therefore I counsel you, lords, leave such doings, that ye write your good deeds in windows or call for God's men [1] when ye give alms, lest ye have your reward here and your heaven also. *Nesciat sinistra quid faciat dextra.* [2] Let not thy left side know, neither late nor early, what thou doest with thy right side, for thus the gospel biddeth that good men should do their alms. Mayors and officers [3] are the means between the King and the Commons to guard the laws, and to punish in pillories and on stools of punishment, brewers and bakers, butchers and cooks ; for these are the men on earth that do most harm to the poor people who buy in small portions. For they often poison the people privily, and they grow rich through their small trade,[4] and get revenue [5] for themselves with what the poor people should put in their belly. Had they made their wealth in honesty they had not built such high houses nor bought such tenements for themselves, [6] be ye full certain.

[1] That is, send for the friars.
[2] Let not your left hand know what your right hand doeth.
[3] Lit. *mace-bearers, i.e.,* officers of the courts of justice.
[4] *I.e.,* retail trade.
[5] *Rentes* = that which is rendered in return for investments.
[6] See Appendix, p. 117, for additional lines of C.

But Meed the Maid hath besought the Mayor to take from all such sellers silver, or presents without pence, whether cups of silver, rings, or other riches, to maintain these dealers. "For my love," said the lady, "love each of them, and suffer them to sell somewhat against reason."

Solomon the Wise made a sermon for amendment of mayors and men who guard the laws, and told them this matter that I think to tell; *Ignis devorabit tabernacula eorum qui libenter accipiunt munera*, etc.[1] Among learned men this Latin meaneth that fire shall fall, and burn all to blue ashes the houses and the homes of them that desire gifts or year-gifts[2] because of their office.

Now the King came from his council and called for Meed, and sent for her very quickly with many officers, who brought her to the chamber joyfully.

Then the King spoke courteously to Meed the Maid, and said these words :

"Woman, unwisely thou hast often done, but worse didst thou never than when thou tookest Falsehood. But I forgive thee that guilt and grant thee my favour ; henceforth, to thy day of death,

---

[1] Fire shall devour the tabernacles of those who have willingly received gifts (bribery).

[2] A *year-gift* is a toll or fine taken by the King's officers on a person's entering an office, and is really a bribe given to them to connive at extortion or other offences in him who gives it. (*Skeat.*)

do so no more. [1]   I have a knight, Conscience, who.
hath lately come from over-sea ; [2] if he desire thee
to wife, wilt thou have him ? "

"Yea, lord," said the lady.   "Lord forbid otherwise ; except I be wholly at your bidding, let hang
me soon ! "

And then Conscience was called to come and
appear before the King and his Council, such
as clerks and others.   Conscience made obeisance to the King, and kneeled, that he might
know what his will might be, and what he should
do.

"Wilt thou wed this woman ? " said the King,
"if I will assent, for she is eager for thy fellowship,
to be thy mate ? "

Said Conscience to the King, "Christ forbid it
me ! Ere I wed such a wife, woe betide me !
For her faith is frail and her speech fickle, and ⁄
she maketh men do wrong many a score of times.
Trust in her treasure vexeth full many.   She
teacheth wantonness to wives and widows, and
lechery to them who love her gifts ; she made
your father fall through false promises, and she
hath poisoned popes and injured Holy Church.
By Him who made me there is not a better bawd
between heaven and hell, though men sought it

---

[1] C. adds : "If thou be again taken in offence, I will shut
thee up as if thou wert an anchorite, in the Castle of Corfe
or a much worse dwelling, and mar thee with torture, by
St. Mary, so that all wanton women shall beware because of
thee."   [2] Lit., "beyond."

on earth.   For she is changeful with her person,
tale-bearing with her tongue, as common as a cart- ✓
way to every knave that walks, to monks, to
minstrels, to lepers in hedges.   Sizers and summoners, such the men who praise her, and if she
were not, the sheriffs of shires were undone.   For
she maketh men lose both their land and life, and
she letteth prisoners go and often payeth for them,
and giveth the jailors both gold and groats, if they
will unfetter the wicked to flee where it pleaseth
him ; and she taketh the true man by the hair and
tieth him fast, and for hatred doth hang him who
never did harm.   She careth not a rush to be
cursed in court, for she doth clothe the commissary
and his clerks ; she is absolved as soon as it pleaseth
her, and can do nigh as much in one single month
as your private seal in six score days.   For she is
familiar with the Pope, as provisors know, for Sir
Simony and herself seal their bulls.   She blesseth
the bishops though they be ignorant, provideth
parsons with prebends, and abetteth priests in
having lovers and concubines all their days, and
in bringing forth children against the law's command.   Where she is well with the King woe is
the kingdom, for she favoureth the false and often
revileth Truth.   By Jesus ! with her jewels she
corrupteth your Justices and lieth against the law,
and stoppeth up the way so that Loyalty cannot
go forward, because her florins are so thick.   She
conducteth the law as she listeth and maketh

love-days,[1] and causeth men to lose through her love what law could win ; it is confusion for a poor man though he plead for ever here. Law is so lordly and loath to make an end : without presents or pence she pleaseth very few.

" She bringeth barons and burgesses into sorrow, and all the commons who wish to live honestly into trouble ; she coupleth together learning and avarice. This is the life of that lady ! Now the Lord give her sorrow ! And all that help her servants, ill-luck betide them ! For poor men, though they suffer, have no power to complain, Meed is such a master among men of wealth."

Then Meed bemoaned, and complained to the King, and prayed to have space to speak, if she might so speed.

The King with a good will granted her grace : " Excuse thee, if thou canst, I can say no more, for Conscience accuseth thee to rid himself of thee for ever."

" Nay, lord," the lady said, " trust him the less when ye know indeed where the wrong lieth. Meed can help where is great misfortune. And thou knowest, Conscience, I have come not to strive, nor with a proud heart to revile thy person.

---

[1] *Love-day,* " commonly meant a law-day, a day set apart for a leet or manorial court, a day of final *concord* and *reconciliation*" (quoted by Prof. Skeat, from Timb's " Nooks and Corners of English Life "). But it is clear that on such occasions much injustice was frequently done to the poor. (*Skeat.*)

Well thou dost know, deceiver, except thou wilt lie, that thou hast hung on my side eleven times, and seized also my gold and given it where thou hast pleased; and why thou art angry now is a wonder to me. According to my power I may still honour thee with gifts, and uphold thy manhood more than thou knowest. But thou hast foully defamed me here before the King, for I never killed any king, nor counselled it, nor did as thou deemest. I call the King to witness![1]

" In Normandy for my sake he was not harmed;[2] but thou thyself truly often shamedst him; thou didst creep into a cabin against the cold in thy nails, and didst think that winter would have lasted for ever, and didst dread thou wouldst die for a dim cloud, and didst hie homeward for thy belly's hunger. Without pity, thief, thou didst rob poor men and didst bear their brass on thy

[1] See Appendix, p. 117, for additional lines of C.

[2] This alludes to Edward III.'s wars in Normandy and to the treaty of Bretigny, signed May 8, 1360. Edward there renounced his claim to the crown of France, and the greater part of his so-called possessions in that country. He also restored all his conquests except Calais and Guisnes. The Dauphin of France promised to pay a ransom of three million crowns of gold for the ransom of his father, King John.

" The sufferings of the English in their previous retreat from Paris to Bretagne were very great, and they encountered a most dreadful tempest near Chartres, with violent wind and heavy hail. Hence the allusions in the text to the lengthening out of winter till May, to the dim cloud, and to the famine from which the army suffered. Meed suggests that instead of exacting money, Edward should have foregone it, or even have paid some, to secure to himself the kingdom of France." (*Skeat.*)

back to sell at Calais ; whereas I stayed here with my lord to save his life ; I made his men merry and stopped their mourning and patted them on their back and emboldened their hearts, and made them dance for hope that they might have me. Had I been marshal of his men, by Mary of Heaven, I durst have laid my life, and no less a pledge, he should have been lord of that land in length and breadth, and also king of that country and of power to help his kin,—the least child of his blood a baron's peer ! But thou, Conscience, cowardlike, didst counsel him to go hence, and for a little silver to leave his lordship, that is the richest realm over which the rain hovereth.

" It becometh a king who doth care for a king-dom to give Meed to men who serve him humbly, and to honour aliens and all men with gifts. Meed maketh him beloved and held as a man. Emperors and earls, and every kind of lord, have young men to run and ride, because of gifts ; the Pope and all prelates receive presents, and themselves meed men to maintain their laws. We see full truly servants for their service take Meed from their master, according as they may agree ; beggars in their begging ask Meed of men; minstrels for their mirth ask Meed ; the King to keep peace in the land hath Meed from his men ; men that teach children crave Meed for them ; priests that preach to the people for good, ask Meed, or pence for masses, and their meat at meal-times ; crafts-

6

men of every kind crave Meed for their prentices ;
merchants and Meed must needs go together ; no
creature can live without Meed, I ween." [1]

The King said to Conscience, "By Christ,
methinketh Meed is well worthy to have the
mastery." [1]

" Nay," said Conscience to the King, and kneeled
on the earth, "there are two kinds of Meed, my ✓
lord, by your leave. The one, God of His grace,
granteth in His bliss to those that do well while
they are here. The prophet preacheth thereof
and putteth it in the Psalter ; *Domine, quis habitabit
in tabernaculo tuo ?* [2] 'Lord, who shall dwell in
Thy habitations and with Thy holy saints, or rest
in Thy holy hills ?'   David asketh this ; and
explaineth it himself, as the Psalter saith ; *Qui
ingreditur sine macula et operatur justiciam,* [3] Those
that enter spotless [4] and of one will, and have
wrought works of right and reason : and he that
followeth not the life of usury, and teacheth poor
men and pursueth truth ; *qui pecuniam suam non
dedit ad usuram, et munera super innocentem,* [5] etc.,
and all that help the innocent and hold with the
righteous, and do them good without Meed and
help the truth,—such kind of men, my lord, shall

---

[1] See Appendix, p. 119, for additional lines in C.
[2] Lord, who shall dwell in Thy tabernacle?
[3] Whoso enters without spot and works justice.
[4] Lit., " of one colour."
[5] Whoso hath not given his money to the usurer and received
gifts against the innocent.

have from God this first Meed at their great need when they go hence.

"There is another unrighteous [1] Meed that masters desire ; they take Meed to abet misdoers ; and thereof the Psalter says at the end of a psalm, *In quorum manibus iniquitates sunt, dextera eorum repleta est muneribus,*[2] and he that graspeth at her gold, so God help me, shall pay for it bitterly, or the Book lieth. Priests and parsons that desire pleasure and take Meed and money for the masses they sing, have their Meed here, as Matthew teacheth us ; *Amen, amen, receperunt mercedem suam.*[3] What labourers and humble folk receive from their masters is no kind of Meed but a rightful hire. In trading there is no Meed, I can well avow ; it is plainly an exchange, one penny-worth for another. But thou, recreant Meed, didst thou never read *Regum*[4] why the vengeance fell on Saul and on his children ? God sent to Saul by Samuel the prophet that Agag of Amalek and all his people must die for a deed their fathers had done. 'Therefore,' Samuel said to Saul, 'God himself commanded thee be obedient to His bidding and fulfil His will. Go to Amalek with thine host, and whatsoever thou findest there, slay it ; burn to death men and beasts, widows

---

[1] Lit., "measureless."
[2] In whose hands are iniquities, whose right hand is full of gifts.
[3] Verily, verily, they have received their reward.
[4] (The Book) of Kings.

and wives, women and children, goods of every
kind ;[1] and all that thou canst find, burn it, bear
it not away for Meed nor money, though it be
never so rich ; see thou destroy it, kill and spare
not, and thou shalt speed the better.' And because
he coveted their cattle, and spared the king, and
forbore to kill both him and his beasts, otherwise
than he was warned of the prophet, as the Bible
witnesseth, God said to Samuel that Saul should
die, and for that sin all his seed come to a
shameful end. Such ruin Meed made Saul the
King to have, so that God hated him and all his
heirs for ever after. The *culorum*[2] of this matter
I care not to show ; in case it should vex men I
will make no end. For it is ever the way of the
world with them that have power, that whosoever
saith the truth to them is soonest blamed.

" I, Conscience, know this, for Mother-wit taught
me it, that Reason shall reign and govern kingdoms ; and just as to Agag it happened so it shall
to some others. Samuel shall slay him and Saul
shall be blamed and David shall be crowned and
subdue them all ; and one Christian king shall
rule them all. Meed shall no more be master, as
she is now, but Love and Lowliness and Loyalty
shall together be masters on earth to save Truth.
And whosoever trespasseth against Truth or goeth

---

[1] Lit., "moveables and unmoveables."
[2] Conclusion. Evidently a corruption of *saeculorum*, the last
word of the *Gloria Patri.* (*Skeat.*)

against his will, Loyalty shall give him law and no
man else. No serjeant shall wear a silken coif for
his service, nor fur on his cloak for pleading at the
bar. Meed maketh of evil-doers many lords, and
ruleth the kingdoms in despite of lords' laws.

" But Love [1] and Conscience shall come together,
and make a labourer of Law ; for such love shall
arise, and such peace among the people, and such
perfect truth, that the Jews shall wax wondrous
glad, and think in their minds that Moses or Messiah
be come to the earth, and shall wonder in their
hearts that men be so true.

" All who bear a baselard,[2] broad sword or lance,
or an axe or a hatchet or any other weapon, shall
be doomed to death except he cause it to be
smithied into a sickle or a scythe or a ploughshare
or a coulter ; *conflabunt gladios suos in vomeres,*[3]
&c. ; and every man shall busy himself with a
plough, or with pickaxe or spade, shall spin or
spread dung or else must he waste himself in sloth.
Priests and parsons shall hunt with *placebo* [4] or
ding upon David [5] every day till evening, and if
any of them shall hunt or hawk, the benefice that

---

[1] The original word here is *kynde love*, *i.e.*, lit., natural or
human love.

[2] A special kind of sword.

[3] They shall melt their swords into ploughshares.

[4] Lit., "I will please," or "find favour with." The opening
phrase of Psa. cxvi. 9. · *To hunt with placebo* = to be dili-
gent in singing *placebo*, *i.e.*, in saying the office for the dead.
(*Skeat.*)

[5] *Dyngen upon David*, *i.e.*, to practise singing the Psalms.

was his boast shall then be taken from him. Neither king nor knight, constable nor mayor, shall override the commons, nor summon them to the Court, nor empanel them [1] to make them pledge their truth, but judgment shall be given according to the deed that is done, pardon or no pardon as Truth will agree.   King's Court and Common Court, Consistory and Chapter, all shall be but one court and one baron be Justice ; and he shall be True-tongue, an honest man who never vexed me.   No battles shall there be, nor shall any man bear weapon, and if any smith shall smithy a weapon he shall be therewith smitten to death.   *Non levabit gens contra gentem gladium,* [2] &c.   But ere this good fortune come to pass men shall feel the worst, by six suns and a ship and half a sheaf of arrows ; and the middle of a moon shall convert the Jews, and Saracens shall sing *Gloria in excelsis* [3] because of that sight, for ill hap at that time shall befall Mahomet and Meed. [4]   For, *melius est bonum nomen quam diuicie multe."* [5]

---

[1] Lit., "put them on a panel."   "The *pannel* of a jury is the slip of parchment on which the names of the jurors are written " (*Wedgwood,* quoted by Skeat).

[2] Nation shall not raise sword against nation.

[3] Glory in the highest.

[4] The whole of this passage is a fanciful prophecy which hints at a final time when Jews and Mahometans shall be converted. Professor Skeat thus explains it : "The Paschal full moon (with the events of the crucifixion) shall cause the Jews to be converted to Christianity ; and next, at the sight of their conversion, Saracens also shall declare their belief in the Holy Ghost ; for both Mohammed and Meed shall then meet with ill-success."   [5] Better is a good name than much riches.

Then Meed waxed as wroth as the wind. " I can no Latin," said she, " clerks know the truth. See what Solomon saith in the Books of Wisdom, that they who give gifts win the victory, and he had much worship for it, as Holy Writ telleth. *Honorem adquiret qui dat munera,*" &c. [1]

" I believe, indeed, lady," said Conscience, " that thy Latin is true ; but thou art like a lady who read a lesson once, and it was *omnia probate,*[2] and that pleased her heart, for no more was there of that line at the leaf's end. If she had looked the other side, and turned the leaf, she would have found many words following thereon, *quod bonum est tenete.*[3] Truth made that text. And so did ye fare, Madam ! Ye could find no more though ye looked on Wisdom when ye sat in study. This text that ye have said, would be good for lords, but a clever clerk ye needed, to have turned the leaf ! And if ye look at Wisdom again ye shall find what followeth, a full harmful text to them who take Meed, and that is *Animam autem aufert accipientium,*[4] &c., and that is the end of that text that ye before showed—that though with Meed we may win worship and victory, the soul that taketh the gift by so much is it bound." [5]

---

[1] He shall win honour who giveth gifts.
[2] Prove all things.
[3] Hold fast that which is good.
[4] For he wins the soul (good will) of the receivers (of gifts).
[5] *I.e.*, the man who takes the gift is to that extent under an obligation.

PASSUS IV.

The King orders Reason to be sent for—He comes with Wit and Wisdom—The petition of Peace against Wrong, who tries to buy off Peace with Meed's help—Reason is relentless and counsels the King to act with justice—The King agrees, and asks Reason to stay with him for ever.

"CEASE," the King said, " I will no longer suffer you ; ye shall be reconciled, forsooth, and both serve me.   Kiss her, Conscience, I bid you," said the King.

" Nay," said Conscience, " by Christ, dismiss me for ever !   Save Reason counsel me thereto, rather will I die ! "

Then the King said to Conscience, "I command thee hasten to ride and fetch Reason ; command him that he come to hear my counsel, for he shall rule my kingdom and advise me for the best, and shall reckon with thee, Conscience, how thou dost teach the people, both learned and unlearned—so Christ help me ! "

" I am glad of that agreement," the man then said, and he rideth straight to Reason and whispereth in his ear, and said as the King bade, and then took his leave.

48

" Tarry thou awhile," said Reason, " I will make
me ready to ride " ; and he called Cato his servant,
who was courteous of speech, and also Tom-true-
tongue-tell-me-no-tales-nor-idle-stories-to-laugh-at-
for-I-loved-them-never. And saddle me Suffer-
till-I-see-my-time, and gird him well with the
girths of Wise-word, and hang upon him the
heavy bridle to keep his head low, for he will
neigh twice [1] ere he be there."

Then Conscience goeth forward fast upon his
horse, and Reason rideth with him, and they talk
together of all the tyrannies Meed causeth upon
the earth. One Waryn Wisdom and his companion
Witty [2] followed fast upon them, for they had
business in hand in the Exchequer and in
Chancery ; and they rode fast that Reason might
advise them the best, and, for silver, save them
from shame and trouble. And Conscience knew
well that they loved Covetousness, and he bade
Reason ride fast and reck of neither of them.
" There are wiles in their words and they dwell with
Meed, and where wrath and wrangling are there
they win silver, but where are love and loyalty
they will not come. *Contricio et infelicitas in vijs
eorum,*[3] &c. They care not one goose wing for
God, *non est timor dei ante oculos corum.*[4] For
God knoweth they would do more for a dozen

[1] *I.e.*, be impatient.
[2] Witty = clever or crafty.
[3] Sorrow and unhappiness are in their ways.
[4] The fear of God is not before their eyes.

chickens, or as many capons, or for a horse-load of oats, than for love of our Lord or of all His dear saints. Therefore, Reason, let those rich folk ride alone, for neither Conscience nor Christ knoweth them, as I trow." So then Reason rode fast on the straight highway, as Conscience showed him, till they came to the King.

Then the King came courteously to meet Reason, and set him on the bench between him and his son, and they talked together very wisely a great while.

And then Peace came into Parliament and put forth a petition, how that Wrong had taken his wife against his will, and had ravished of their maidenhood Rose, Reginald's love, and Margaret, in spite of their checks. "His fellows steal both my geese and my pigs, and for fear of him I dare not fight nor complain.[1] He borrowed a horse of me and he never brought him home, nor any far- thing for him, for. aught I can plead. He abetteth his men in murdering my servants, he forestalleth my sales[2] at fairs, and wrangleth in my market, and breaketh away my barn door and beareth off my wheat, and giveth me nothing but a tally[3] for

[1] C. adds : " In faith, because of his men I dare not bear any silver in safety to St. Giles' Down. Full well he watcheth when I take silver, and right eagerly he espieth which way I go, that he may rob and rifle me if I ride softly."

[2] To *forestall*, was to buy up goods before they had been exposed in the market. It was strictly discouraged. (*Skeat.*)

[3] The tally was a wooden stick, one of a pair that *tallied*, with notches in it to indicate the sum lent or owing.

ten quarters of oats, and he beateth me also and lieth by my maid, I hardly dare look about me because of him."

The King knew he said the truth, for Conscience told him that Wrong was a wicked fellow and wrought much sorrow. Then Wrong was afraid, and he sought Wisdom that with his pence he might make peace, and offered him much pence and said, "If I had the favour of my Lord the King little would I reck, though Peace and all his power complained to him for ever."

Then Wisdom and Sir Waryn the Witty, because Wrong had wrought so wicked a deed, went and warned Wrong with this wise talk: "Whoso worketh after his own will often causeth wrath, I say it concerning thyself, thou shalt indeed find it so. Except Meed manage it thy ruin is certain, for in his favour lie both thy life and thy land."

Then Wrong wooed Wisdom very eagerly, and that he might make peace with his pence paid *handy dandy*;[1] and then Wisdom and Wit went together, and took Meed with them, to get pardon for Wrong.

Peace came forth with a bloody pate. "Without guilt, God wot, gat I this hurt; Conscience and the Commons know the truth."

But Wisdom and Wit wrought diligently to overcome the King with money, if they could.

---

[1] An allusion to the children's game of "Which hand will you have?" The word here means a secret bribe. (*Skeat.*)

The King swore both by Christ and his crown that Wrong should suffer punishment for his deeds, and commanded a constable to put him in irons, "And let him not see his feet once these seven years."

"God wot," said Wisdom, "that were not the best. If he can make amends let Bail have him ; and be surety for his wrong, and buy him a remedy, and so amend what is ill-done, and be the better evermore."

Wit agreed thereto and said the same. "Better is it for Redress [1] to overcome Wrong,[2] than for Wrong to be beaten and Redress be none the better off."

Then Meed humbled herself and besought for mercy, and offered Peace a present of pure gold. "Take this, man, from me," she said, "to amend thine hurt, for I will be surety for Wrong he will do so no more."

Then Peace piteously besought the King to have mercy on the man who so often had wrought him ill, "For he hath given me good surety as Wisdom hath taught him, and with a good will I forgive him that guilt, and if the King assent I cannot say further ; for Meed hath made me amends, I can ask no more."

"Nay," said the King then, "so Christ help me, Wrong goeth not thus away, I will first know more ; for he would laugh if he should escape so

---

[1] Lit., boot or remedy.   [2] Lit., bale or evil.

easily, and be afterwards the bolder to beat my
servants; except Reason have pity on him he shall
stay in my stocks, and that as long as he liveth,
except Lowliness be his surety."

Certain men then advised Reason to have pity
on that shrew, and also to counsel thus the King
and Conscience, and they besought Reason that
Meed might be bail.

"Counsel me not to have pity," said Reason,
"Till lords and ladies all love truth, and all hate
harlotry, either to hear or speak it, and till Pernel's[1]
finery be put in her box, and the cherishing[2] of
children become chastisement with rods, and harlots' holiness be held worth a hind;[3] till clerks
be covetous to clothe and feed the poor, and
monks on pilgrimage[4] say *recordare*[5] in their
cloisters as St. Benedict, Bernard, and Francis
commanded; and till preachers' preaching be
proved on themselves; till the King's counsel be the
common profit; till bishops' horses become beggars' chambers,[6] and their hawks and their hounds

[1] A proverbial name for a gaily dressed, bold-faced woman
(*Skeat.*)

[2] *I.e.*, over-indulgence or spoiling.

[3] *I.e.*, of small value, of common occurrence. A hind or
farm-labourer was not of great value. *Harlot* in M. Eng. is
applied both to men and women; and is often used in the sense
of *ribald*, rather than in its modern meaning.

[4] Lit., "religious," any one of a religious order.

[5] "Remember"; the first word of a Mass for avoiding sudden
death.

[6] *I.e.*, Till the money spent by bishops on horses go to furnish
rooms for beggars.

help the poor Orders; and till St. James be sought where I shall show [1] so that no man go to Galicia except he go for ever; and until all runners to Rome bear across the sea no silver that has upon it the King's image, to enrich robbers who dwell yonder; neither gold nor silver graven nor un-graven, on pain of forfeiture if any man find him at Dover, except it be a merchant or his man, or a messenger with letters, or a provisor or a priest, or a penitent for his sins.

"And still," said Reason, "by the Rood, I will have no pity while Meed hath the mastery in this judgment hall; but I can point out examples as at times I see them. As for myself," he said, "if so it were that I were a crowned king to guard a realm, never should wrong in this world, that I could know, be unpunished as far as in me lay, for my soul's peril! Nor my favour got by gifts, so God save me, nor pardon be had for Meed except through Meekness. For the man *nullum malum* met with *inpunitum*, and bade *nullum bonum* be *irremuneratum*. [2] Let your confessor, Sir King, explain this without help of gloss; [3] and if ye fulfil it in deeds, I pledge mine ears that that Law shall be a labourer and carry dung a-field, and Love shall rule thy land as shall please thee best."

[1] The C-text has, "Till St. James be sought where the poor sick lie, in prisons and poor cots, instead of pilgrimage to Rome."

[2] The man named *No evil* met with one called *Unpunished*, and bade *No Good* be *unrewarded*. This is a fantastic way of introducing the words in italics.   [3] Commentary.

Then clerks who were confessors joined together to interpret this clause, and for the King's profit, but not for the Commons' comfort nor for the King's soul. For in the judgment hall, I saw Meed wink upon the men of law, and they went to her laughing, and many left Reason.

Waryn Wisdom winked at Meed and said, "Madam, I am your man, whatsoever my mouth may prate about; I light upon florins," said he, "and often then speech faileth me."

All the just then declared that Reason said truth, and Wit agreed thereto and commended his words, and so did most in the hall, and many of the crowd, and they held Meekness as a master and Meed a cursed shrew. Love held her lightly and Loyalty thought still less of her, and proclaimed it so loudly that all the hall heard it. "Whosoever for the wealth of her goods desireth her to wife, except he be known for a cuckold cut off my nose!"

Then Meed bemoaned and made heavy cheer, because the lowest in the court called her a whore. But a sizer and a summoner quickly followed her, and a sheriff's clerk cursed all the rout. "For often," said he, "I have helped you at the Bar, and yet ye never gave me the worth of a rush."

And the King called Conscience, and then Reason, and declared that Reason had spoken rightly; and the King looked exceeding angrily upon Meed, and waxed wroth with Law because

Meed had almost ruined it, and said, "Through your Law, so I believe, I lose many escheats ; [1] Meed overcometh Law and doth hinder Truth greatly. But Reason shall reckon with you, if I reign any time ; and, even as to-day, he shall judge you as ye have deserved. Meed shall not bail you, by the Mary of Heaven ! I will have loyalty in Law and stop all your idle talk, and as most men witness plainly so shall Wrong be judged."

Said Conscience to the King, "Except the Commons will agree, it is full hard, by my head, to bring this about, and thus to rule your liege people fairly."

"By Him who hung upon the Rood," said Reason to the King, "except I rule your realm thus, tear me to pieces ! if ye but command Obedience to be with me."

"And I agree," said the King, "by St. Mary my Lady, when my council of clerks and earls is come ; but thou shalt not lightly depart from me, Reason, for as long as I live I will never let thee go."

"I am ready to abide for ever with you," said Reason, " so long as Conscience be of our council, I care for nothing better."

"And I grant it," said the King ; " God forbid it should fail ; as long as our life doth last let us live together ! " [2]

[1] Property reverting to the King.
[2] See Appendix, pp. 120–125, for the C. passages which now follow.

PASSUS V.

The Dreamer awakes, but sleeps again—He sees the Field, and Reason preaching—Reason's sermon—The confession of the Seven Deadly Sins, and the Repentance of Robert the Robber —Repentance prays for all of them—They all set out to find Truth, but none know the way—Piers the Plowman says he will show them, and describes the way.

THE King and his knights went to church to hear the Matins of the day, and afterwards the Mass. Then I awoke from my sleep, and was withal sorrowful that I had not slept more soundly and seen more. But before I had gone a furlong faintness seized me, so that I might not go a foot further for sleep ; and I sat softly down and said my Belief, and as I babbled on my beads they sent me to sleep.

And then saw I much more than I have told before, for I saw the field full of folk that I before spoke of, and how Reason got himself ready to preach to all the realm, and with a cross began his sermon thus before the King :—

He proved that the pestilences were for sin alone, and also the south-west wind on Saturday at evening was plainly for pride alone, and nothing

else.   Pear trees and plum trees were blown to
the earth, for warning, ye should do better, ye
men.   Beeches and broad oaks were blown to the
ground, and their roots turned upwards, in token
of fear that deadly sin at Doomsday shall destroy
them all.

Of this matter I might mumble on full lengthily,
but I will say as I saw, so God help me, how
plainly Reason preached before the people.   He
bade the waster go do what he best could, and
make good his wasting by some kind of craft.
And he prayed Pernel to let be her finery, and
keep it in her box for her use in need.   Tom
Stowe he told to take two staves, and fetch Felice
home from the women's punishment.[1] He warned
Wat that his wife was blameworthy, and that her
head was worth half a mark and his hood not
worth a groat.   And he bade Bat cut a bough or
two, and beat Beton therewith, unless she would
work.   And then he charged chapmen to chasten
their children, " And let no indulgence spoil them
while they are young, nor even for any attack of
pestilence please them out of reason.   My father
said to me, and so did my mother, that ' to the

---

[1] A difficult passage, explained in various ways, but Prof.
Skeat's opinion is as follows :—" I suppose the sentence to
mean that Tom Stowe, who had neglected his wife and let her
get into bad ways, or who had allowed her to be punished as a
scold, had much better fetch her home than leave her exposed
to public derision.   Such an errand would require a strong arm,
and two staves would be very useful in dispersing the crowd."

dearer child the more teaching is needful.' And
Solomon who wrote Wisdom said the same, *Qui
parcit virge, odit filium.* The English of this Latin
—if any will know it—is, ' Whoso spareth the rod
spoileth his children.' "

And next he besought both prelates and priests,
" What ye preach to the people prove it on
yourselves, and do it in deeds, and it shall bring
good to you ; for if ye live as ye teach us we shall
believe you the better."

And then he counselled the Orders of religion
to keep their rule, " Lest the King and his council
lessen your allowance, and become stewards of
your houses till ye be ordered better." [1] And
afterwards he counselled the King to love the
Commons. " They are thy treasure, if treason
should be ; and thy remedy in need." And then
he prayed the Pope to have pity on Holy Church,
and ere he give any grace let him first govern
himself. " And ye that have laws to guard let
Truth be what ye covet more than gold or other
gifts, if ye will please God ; for whoso is contrary
to Truth He telleth us in the Gospel that God doth
not know him, nor any saint in Heaven. *Amen
dico vobis, nescio vos.*[2] And ye who seek St. James,
and the saints of Rome, seek St. Truth, for he can
save you all ; *Qui cum patre et filio* [3] that it may be

---

[1] See Appendix, p. 125, for C. passage.
[2] Verily I say to you, I know you not.
[3] Who with the Father and the Son, &c.

well with them who follow my sermon." And thus said Reason.

Then came Repentance and repeated Reason's theme, and made Will [1] weep water with his eyes.

Superbia (Pride).

Pernel Proud-heart threw herself to the earth, and lay long ere she looked up, and cried, " Lord, mercy ! " and vowed to Him who made us all that she would unsew her shift and put upon her a hair shirt, to tame her flesh, that was fierce to sin. " High heart shall never seize me, but I will hold me low and suffer myself to be spoken ill of ; and thus have I never done before. But now I will be meek and beseech pardon, for all this I have hated in my heart." [2]

Luxuria (Lechery).

Then Lecher said " Alas ! " and he cried on our Lady for mercy between God and his soul because of his misdeeds,—if that he should drink only with the duck, and dine but once on Saturdays for seven years after.

Invidia (Envy).

Envy with heavy heart asked for shrift, and

---

[1] This may refer to the author ; but, more likely, the term "Will" is used, as in Bunyan's Lord Will-be-will, for the *will* in the sense of the whole emotional and passionate nature.

[2] See Appendix, p. 127, for passage in C.

sorrowfully he began to cry out *mea culpa.*[1] He
was as pale as a pellet,[2] and seemed in the palsy,
and he was clothed in a caurimawry,[3] which I
could not describe. He was in kirtle[4] and
kourteby[5] and a knife by his side, the upper
sleeves were of a friar's frock. And like a leek
which had lain long in the sun, so he looked, with
his hollow cheeks and evil scowl. His body was
nigh swollen to bursting for anger, so that he bit
his lips, and he went along clenching his fist, and
thought to avenge himself in deeds or in words
when he saw his time. Every word he threw out
was from an adder's tongue ; he lived by finding
fault and making accusation, together with backbiting and slander and bearing false witness ;
this was all his courtesy wherever he showed
himself.

"I would be shriven," said this shrew, "if for
shame I durst : by God, I would be gladder for
Gib to have ill-luck than if I had this week
won a wey[6] of Essex cheese. I have a neighbour
nigh me, I have often vexed him, and lied about
him to lords to make him lose his silver, and I
have made his friends be his foes through my

[1] My sin, *i.e.*, "I have sinned," a phrase taken from the
form of confession. The C-text adds here, "His clothes were of
cursing and sharp words."
[2] A pellet or ball used as a war-missile, generally of stone.
[3] The name of some coarse, rough material.
[4] A kind of under-jacket.
[5] A short coat or cloak.
[6] *Wey* = A certain weight, here 3 cwt.

false tongue.   His favour and his good fortune full sorely grieve me.

"Between house and house I often make strife, so that both life and limb are lost through my words.   And when I meet in the market him whom I most hate, I hail him graciously as if I were his friend, for he is stronger than I, and I dare do no other.   But had I mastery and might, —God knoweth my will !

"And when I come to the church, and should kneel to the Rood, and pray for the people as the priest teacheth, for pilgrims and palmers and afterwards for all people, then I ask on my knees that Christ may give them sorrow who bore away my bowl and my tattered sheet.[1]   I turn my eyes away from the altar and see how Ellen has a new coat, and I wish then it were mine, and all the web it came from.   And I laugh at men's loss, for it pleaseth my heart, and I weep at their gain and bewail the time, and deem that they do ill when I do full worse ; and whoso reproveth me for it I bear him deadly hate afterwards.   I would that every man were my servant, for when any hath more than I it sorely vexeth me.   And thus I live loveless like an evil dog, and all my body swelleth for the bitterness of my gall.[2]   I have not eaten as

[1] The bowl was probably a large wooden one, used to contain scraps of broken victuals.   Neither bowl nor sheet was a thing of any value, but Envy could not refrain from cursing the thief. (*Skeat.*)
[2] See Appendix, p. 129, for C. passage.

a man ought for many years, for envy and evil will are hard to digest. Can no sugar, nor sweet thing assuage my swelling ? nor no *diapenidion* [1] drive it from my heart, nor neither shrift nor shame, except one scrape my maw ? "

" Yes, readily," said Repentance, and counselled him for the best, " Sorrow for sins is salvation of souls."

" I am sorry," said Envy, " I am but seldom otherwise, and it maketh me thus thin because I cannot avenge me. Among burgesses in London I have been dwelling, and bade Backbiting be a broker to find fault with men's wares. When he sold and I not, then was I ready to lie and scowl on my neighbour and to find fault with his goods. I will amend this, if I may, through the might of God Almighty."

Ira (Anger).

Now awaketh Wrath, with two white eyes, and snivelling with his nose, and bending his neck.[2] "I am Wrath," said he, " I was sometime a friar and the convent's gardener for grafting shoots. On limiters [3] and lectors [4] I grafted lies, till they

---

[1] An emollient, or expectorant. Prof. Skeat remarks on the passage—"A forcible way of expressing the question, 'Can none but the most violent measures relieve my moral sickness ? '"

[2] C. has " biting his lips."

[3] Members of a convent licensed to beg within a certain limited district.

[4] One of the orders of clergy.

bore leaves of lowly speech to please lords, and then they blossomed abroad into the lady's bower to hear confession, and there is come this fruit thereof,—that folk would sooner make confession to them than confess to their own parsons. And now the parsons have perceived that these friars share the profits with them, and these *possessioners* [1] preach and slander the friars, and the friars find them in the wrong, as folk bear witness, and say that when they preach to the people in many a place around, I, Wrath, walk with them and teach them from my books. Thus they both speak of spiritual power, so that either despiseth the other, till they become beggars and live by the spiritual power that I give them ; or else they are all rich and ride about. I, Wrath, never rest that I do not follow this wicked folk, for such is my grace. I have an aunt both nun and abbess ; she would sooner swoon or die than suffer any pain. I have been cook in her kitchen and served the convent many months, with them, and also with the monks. I was pottage maker for the prioress and other poor ladies, and made them pottage from the idle talk that Dame Joanna was a bastard, and Dame Clarice was a knight's daughter, but her father was a cuckold, and Dame Pernel a priest's wench, who will never be prioress, for she had a child in cherry-time, all our chapter knew it. I,

---

[1] *Possessioner* probably here means one of the beneficed clergy.

Wrath, dressed their herbs with wicked words, till 'Thou liest,' and 'Thou liest,' leaped out at once, and either hit the other on the cheek ; by Christ, had they had knives each had killed the other ! Saint Gregory was a good Pope, and had good forethought when he ordained that no prioress should be priest.[1] For they then had been *infamis*[2] the first day, so ill can they keep counsel.

"Among monks I might go, but I shun them many a time, because there are many cruel men to spy out my doings, both prior and superior and our *pater abbas ;* and if I tell any tales they consult together and make me fast on Fridays on bread and water, and I am charged in the chapter-house as if I were a child, and chastised on the bare back, without a breech between. So I have no liking to dwell with those men. I eat meagre fish there, and drink weak ale ; but at other times when wine cometh, when I drink at evening, I have a foul mouth full five days afterwards. All the wickedness that I know about any of our brethren I spread it abroad in our cloister, so that all the convent know it."

"Now repent thee," said Repentance, "and do thou never repeat counsel that thou knowest, by

[1] An allusion to the practice of certain abbesses who took upon themselves to hear confession of their nuns as well as " to exercise some other smaller parts of the clerical function."

[2] Infamous ; here refers to the violation of the oath of secrecy in confession.

favour nor by right ; nor drink over-delicate drinks, nor too deep either, lest thy will, because of it, should turn to wrath. ' *Esto sobrius*,'[1] he said, and then absolved me, and bade me wish to weep to amend my wickedness."

Avaricia (Covetousness).

And then came Covetousness ; I cannot describe him, so hungry and hollow Sir Harvey looked. He was beetle-browed and also thick-lipped, with two bleared eyes like a blind hag, and like a leathern purse his cheeks lolled about even lower than his chin, and they trembled for eld.[2] And his beard was beslobbered with bacon, like a bondman's. A hood was on his head above a lousy hat, and he was in a tawny coat twelve winters old and full of vermin, and all dirty and torn to rags, and full of creeping lice ; except a louse were a good leaper she could not have walked on that scurvy coat, it was so threadbare.

" I have been covetous," said this caitiff, " I here acknowledge it. For some time I served Sim at the Stile, and was bound his prentice to serve his profit.

" First I learned to lie a leaf or two, to weigh falsely was my first lesson. At my master's bidding I went to the fair at Weyhill and Winchester with many kinds of merchandise, and had the

---

[1] Be sober.   [2] Old age.

grace of Guile not gone with my wares, they had been unsold these seven years, so God help me !

"Then I went among drapers to learn my primer, and to draw the selvage along that seemed the longer. Among the rich striped cloths I did my lesson, and sewed them with a pack needle, and fastened them together, and put them in a press and pinned them therein, till ten or twelve yards were stretched out to thirteen.

"My wife was a weaver and made woollen cloth ; she told the spinners to spin it out ; but the pound that she paid them by weighed a quarter more than my own balance, if a man weighed true.

"I bought her barley malt and she brewed it to sell. Penny ale [1] and pudding ale [2] she poured together for labourers and poor folk, and kept it by itself. The best ale was kept in my room or in my bedchamber, and whoso tasted of it bought it afterwards, a gallon for a groat, no less, God wot ; and yet it came in cupfuls,[3] for my wife did this trick. Rose the Retailer was her rightful name ; she hath been at huckstering all her lifetime. But I swear now, as I thrive, that I will stop that sin, and never weigh falsely nor use bad

---

[1] Common or thin ale.

[2] Probably called so because it was thick like pudding.

[3] Or, by cups at a time. She knew better than to measure it in a gallon measure.

merchandise, but go to Walsingham with my wife, and pray the Rood of Bromholm[1] to bring me out of debt."

" Didst thou ever repent, or make restitution ? " said Repentance.

"Yes," said he. "Once I was lodged with a crowd of chapmen, and I rose up when they were at rest and rifled their bags."

"That was no restitution," said Repentance, "but a robber's theft; thou hadst been more worthy of hanging for that than for all else that thou hast here showed."

" I weened that rifling was restitution," said he, "for I never learned to read in books, and I know no French, in faith, but of the farthest end of Norfolk."

"Usury didst thou ever use in all thy life?" said Repentance.

" Nay, truly," he said, " except in my youth. I learned a lesson amongst Lombards and Jews, how to weigh pence with a weight, and pare down the heaviest, and to lend it[2] for love of the Cross[3] that a pledge might be laid and lost,[4] and such things I wrote down lest he broke his day.

[1] The cross of Bromholm in Norfolk.

[2] *I.e.*, the light coin.

[3] *For love of the Cross* is a clever pun, since *cross* refers frequently to the cross on the back of old coins, and was a slang name for a coin, as in Shakespeare. (*Skeat.*)

[4] By the borrower. The key to the whole passage is to remember that borrowers often gave pledges of much value. (*Skeat.*)

I have more manors through arrears than through
miseretur et comodat. [1]

"I have lent lords and ladies my merchandise,
and been their broker afterward and bought it
myself; exchanges and chevesances,[2] I deal in
such wares, and lend to folk who lose a good
part of every noble; and with Lombards'
letters I took gold to Rome; and I received
it here by tally, and there counted it out less
to them."

"Didst thou ever lend to lords for desire of
their protection?"

"Yea, I have lent to lords who loved me never
afterwards, and have made many a knight both
mercer and draper who never paid for his prentice-
hood a pair of gloves." [3]

"Hast thou pity on poor men who must needs
borrow [4]?"

"I have as much pity on poor men as a pedlar
hath on cats, who would kill them for greed of
their skins if he could catch them."

"Art thou open-handed with meat and drink
amongst thy neighbours?"

"I am held," he said, "as courteous as a cur in

---

[1] He is merciful and lends—a phrase from Psalm cxii. 5.

[2] Agreements about the loan of money.

[3] Avarice, in his dealings with knights, who came to him for
ready money, made them take part of the loan in kind (silk or
cloth)—the money-lenders' regular practice—and he now ironi-
cally calls his customers mercers and drapers who never paid
anything for their apprenticeship.

[4] *I.e.*, buy on credit.

the kitchen, and among my neighbours in special
I have such a name."

"Now except thou soon repent, may God never
give thee grace on this earth to bestow thy goods
well, nor may thine issue after thee have joy of
what thou winnest, nor may thine executors
bestow well the silver that thou dost entrust them
with, and may what was won with wrong be
spent by wicked men.[1] For if I were a friar of
a house where good faith and charity are, I would
not clothe us with thy goods nor repair our
church, nor have a penny of thine for my pittance,
by my soul's health, for the best book in our
house, though the leaves were of exceeding bright
gold, if I knew indeed thou wert such as thou
tellest, or if I could find out that so it was in any
wise. *Seruus es alterius cum fercula pinguia queris,
pane tuo pocius vescere, liber eris.*[2]

"Thou art an unkindly creature. I can not
absolve thee till thou make restitution and reckon
up with all of them, and until Reason hath en-
rolled it in Heaven's register that thou hast made
it good to every man. *Non dimittitur peccatum,
donec restituatur ablatum,* &c.[3] For all who have
aught of thy goods, so God have my truth, shall
be bound at the great Doom to help thee make

---

[1] See Appendix, p. 130, for passage in C-text.
[2] Thou art the slave of another when thou seekest dainty
dishes, eat rather thine own bread, and thou wilt be free.
[3] Thy sin will not be remitted, until the thing carried off is
restored.

restitution. And whoso believeth not this for truth let him look in the Psalter, in *Miserere mei deus,*[1] whether I speak truly, *Ecce enim veritatem dilexisti,* &c.[2] Never shall workman in this world thrive with what thou dost win ; *Cum sancto sanctus eris,*[3] construe me that in English."

Then that wretch fell into despair, and would have hanged himself had not Repentance the rather heartened him, in this manner :

" Have mercy in mind, and beg for it with thy mouth, for God's mercy is more than all His other works ; *Misericordia eius super omnia opera eius,*[4] &c., and all the wickedness in this world that man could do or think is no more to the mercy of God than a gleed in the sea.[5] *Omnis iniquitas quantum ad misericordiam dei, est quasi sintilla in medio maris.*[6] Therefore keep mercy in thy mind and among thy wares, trust to it ; for thou hast no good ground whereof to get thee a cake, except it were with thy tongue or else thy two hands ; for the goods that thou hast got came through nought but falsehood, and as long as thou livest therewith thou payest naught but rather borrowest. And if ever thou knowest not to what, nor to

[1] Have mercy on me, O Lord.
[2] For behold thou hast delighted in truth.
[3] With the holy thou shalt be holy.
[4] His mercy is over all his works.
[5] C. has, " Wicked deeds fare as a spark of fire that fell in mid-Thames and died for a drop of water."
[6] All iniquity is to the mercy of God as a spark in the midst of the ocean.

whom, to make restitution, take it to the bishop, and ask him of his grace to bestow it himself as is best for thy soul. For he shall answer for thee at the great Doom, for thee and for many more that man shall give account. Trust to naught else than what he taught you in Lent, and what he lent you of our Lord's goods to keep you from sin."

Gula (Gluttony).

Now Glutton goeth to shrift, and betaketh him churchward to show his sins. But Beton the brewster bade him good-morrow, and with that asked him, Whitherward would he ?

"To Holy Church," said he, "to hear mass, and afterwards I will be shriven and sin no more."

"I have good ale, gossip," said she : "Glutton, wilt thou try it ?"

"Hast thou at all in thy store any hot spices ?"

"I have pepper and seeds of pæony," said she, "and a pound of garlic, and a farthing's-worth of fennel seed for fasting days."

Then goeth Glutton in and great oaths after him ; Cis the shoemaker [1] sat on the bench, Wat the warrener and his wife also, Tim the tinker and twain of his prentices, Hick the hackney man, [2] and Hugh the needle-seller, Clarice of Cock Lane, and the clerk of the church, Daw the Ditcher, and

---

[1] *Souteresse*, female shoemaker, or seller of shoes.
[2] One who let out horses on hire.

dozen others, Sir Piers of Pridie and Pernel of Flanders,[1] a fiddle player, a ratter, a sweeper of Cheap,[2] a rope-maker, a riding-man,[3] and Rose the dish-maker, Godfrey of Garlickhithe and Griffin the Welshman, and many old clothesmen; and early in the morning, with brave cheer, they all gave to Glutton good ale for fellowship.[4]

Then Clement the cobbler cast off his cloak, and put it for sale at the New Fair;[5] Hick the hackney-man threw down his hood, and bade Bat the butcher be on his side. There were chapmen chosen to value these wares; whoso hath the hood should have amends for the cloak. Two rose up quickly and whispered together, and apart by themselves appraised these pennyworths; and they could not in their conscience agree rightly, till Robin the roper arose for the truth, and named himself umpire to settle the bargain between the three, that there should be no debate. Hick the

---

[1] C. inserts, "A keeper of cattle, a hermit, the hangman of Tyburn and a dozen rascals—porters, pick-purses, and bald tooth-drawers."

[2] A scavenger of West Cheap, or Cheapside.

[3] Redynkyng = one of a class of feudal retainers who held their land by serving their lord on horseback. (*Skeat.*)

[4] *To hansel* = (lit.) for an earnest or pledge.

[5] A game of barter. "It seems that Hikke chose Bette to be his deputy. Then Bette and one appointed by Clement tried to make a bargain, but could not settle it till Robyn was called in as umpire, by whose decision Clement and Hikke had to abide. Hikke obtained the cloak, which was the better article, and Clement was allowed to fill up his cup at Hikke's expense. If either drew back he was to be fined a gallon of ale." (*Skeat.*)

8

hostler had the cloak, in covenant that Clemen should fill the cup, and have Hick the hostler's hood, and hold himself content ; and whoso first repented it should then rise up and pledge Sir Glutton in a gallon of ale. There was laughing and louring, and they cried "Let the cup go round," and so they sat till evensong, and at times they sang, till Glutton had gulped down a gallon and a gill.

He could neither step nor stand until he had his staff, and then he went like a gleeman's dog, sometimes aside, and sometimes behind, as one who layeth nets to catch fowl. And when he drew nigh the door then his eyes grew dim, and he stumbled on the threshold and fell to the ground. Clement the cobbler caught him round the middle to lift him up, and laid him across his knees. But Glutton was a great churl, and heavy to lift, and coughed up a "caudel" in Clement's lap, that the hungriest hound in Hertfordshire durst not lap of that offal, so unlovely it smelt. With all the woe in the world his wife and his daughter bare him home to bed and put him therein ; and after all this excess he had a fit of sloth, so that he slept Saturday and Sunday until the sun went down. Then he awoke from his slumber, and the first word he said was, "Where is the bowl?" Then his wife upbraided him for his wicked living, and also Repentance rebuked him thus :

"Thou hast wrought evil in thy life in words

and works, shrive thee therefore and be ashamed thereof, and declare it with thy mouth."

"I, Glutton," said the man, "confess myself guilty : that I have trespassed with my tongue I cannot tell how often ; sworn 'God's soul' and 'So God help me and halidom' when there was no need, nine hundred times ; and over-eaten myself at supper and sometimes at dinner,[1] so that I, Glutton, brought it up before I had gone a mile, and spilled what might be saved and spent on some hungry one ; I have both eaten and drunken over-delicately on fasting days, and sometimes sat so long there that I slept and ate together. For love of idle tales in taverns, and to drink the more, I dined, and hied to the meat before noon on fasting days."

"This open confession," said Repentance, "shall be for merit to thee."

And then Glutton began to weep and make great mourning for his wicked life that he had lived, and vowed to fast ; "Neither for hunger nor thirst shall fish on Friday enter me till Abstinence, my aunt, hath given me leave ; and yet have I hated her all my life-time."

Accidia (Sloth).

Then came Sloth with two slimy eyes, and all beslobbered. "I must sit," said he, "or else I

---

[1] Lit., "*nones*," which at this time were at noon.

should nap ; I may not stand nor stoop, nor kneel without a stool. Were I abed no ringing would make me rise, except need of nature, until I were ready to dine." With a great sigh he heaved forth *benedicite*, and beat his breast, and stretched himself and groaned, and at last he snored.

"What! awake, man!" said Repentance, "and haste thee to shrift."

"If I should die on this day I should not care ; I know not my *paternoster* perfectly as the priest singeth it, but I know rimes of Robin Hood and Randolph, Earl of Chester, but neither of our Lord nor our Lady the least rime that ever was made. I have made forty vows and forgotten them in the morning; I never performed penance as the priest bade me, nor was I ever yet right sorry for my sins. And if I pray any prayers, except it be in wrath, what I say with my tongue is two miles from my heart.

"Every day, holidays and others, I am busy with idle tales at the alehouse, and at other times in churches ; God's pain and passion I full seldom think on. I never visited sick men nor fettered folk in prison ; I would rather hear of harlotry or the cobblers' summer game,[1] or lying tales to laugh at and belie my neighbour, than all that Mark and Matthew, John, and Luke ever wrote. And vigils and fasting days, all these I let pass and lie in bed

---

[1] *Summer game*, probably the rural May games, which may have been arranged by the Shoemakers' Guild.

in Lent and my leman in my arms, till matins and mass be done, and then I go to the friars ; if I come to *ite, missa est,*[1] I hold myself served. I am not shriven for a long time except sickness force me, not twice in two years, and then upon guess I shrive myself.

" I have been priest and parson more than thirty winters, yet I can neither solfa [2] nor sing, nor read saints' lives ; but I can find a hare in a field or furrow better than I can interpret plainly one clause in *beatus vir* or *beati omnes*,[3] and tell it to my parishioners. I can hold love-days,[4] and hear a reeve's reckoning, but in the Canon or the Decretals[5] I cannot read a line. If I buy and promise to pay, except it be tallied, I forget it as quickly, and if men ask it of me six or seven times I deny it with oaths ; and thus I vex true men ten hundred times. And my servants' wages are a long time behind, grievous is it to hear the reckoning when we make up accounts ; so with ill will and wrath I pay my workmen.

" If any man doth me a benefit, or helpeth me in need, I am unkind towards his courtesy, and

---

[1] The concluding words of the service of the Mass—"Go ; [the congregation] is dismissed."

[2] *Solfa* = to practise singing the scale of notes.

[3] Blessed is the man (Psa. i. or cxii.). Blessed are all (Psa. cxxviii.).

[4] Days for the settlement of disputes by arbitration.

[5] *Canon*, the canon of the Mass. *Decretals*, a collection of popes' edicts and decrees of councils, forming part of the canon law.

cannot understand it; for I have, and have had, something of a hawk's way; I am not lured with love, except there lie aught under the thumb. The kindness that my fellow-Christians showed me of yore, I, Sloth, have forgotten it sixty times since.

"By speech and by sparing of speech I have wasted many a time both flesh and fish, and many other victuals; both bread and ale, butter, milk, and cheese, I have wasted carelessly in my service, till it could serve no man. I wandered about in youth and gave myself to learn naught, and for my foul sloth have been a beggar ever since; '*heu michi, quod sterilem vitam duxi iuvenilem.*'"[1]

"Repentest thou not?" said Repentance, and forthwith he swooned, till *Vigilate*[2] the watcher fetched water from his eyes, and threw it on his face, and cried to him earnestly, and said, "Beware of Despair, who would betray thee. 'I am sorry for my sins,' say thus to thyself, and beat thyself on the breast, and pray for His grace, for there is no guilt so great but His goodness is greater."

Then Sloth sat up and straightway crossed himself, and made a vow before God against his foul sloth. "There shall be no Sunday this seven years except sickness hinder it, that I shall not before day betake me to the dear church, and hear Matins and Mass as if I were a monk. No ale after meat

---

[1] See p. 17.   [2] Be vigilant.

shall keep me thence till I have heard evensong, I vow to the Rood. And also I will repay, if I have as much, all that I have gained wickedly, since I had wit. And though my livelihood fail, I will never cease until every man have his own ere I go hence ; and with the residue and the remnant, by the Rood of Chester, I will seek Truth first before I see Rome."

Robert the Robber looked on *Reddite*,[1] and for that he had nought wherewith to make restitution he wept full sore. But yet the sinful wretch said to himself, " Christ, that didst die upon the cross on Calvary, when Dismas [2] my brother besought thy grace, and hadst mercy on that man for sake of *memento*,[3] so have pity on this robber who may not have *reddere*,[4] nor may never hope to earn by handicraft what I owe. But for thy great mercy I beseech compassion ; condemn me not at Doomsday for what I did so ill."

What befell this thief I cannot fully show, well I know he wept water fast with both his eyes, and soon after acknowledged his sin to Christ, and vowed that he would polish anew his staff *penitencia*,[5] and go [6] with it on pilgrimage over the land all his life.

---

[1] Restore.
[2] The name of the penitent thief as given in the apocryphal Gospel of Nicodemus.
[3] " Remember." " Domine *memento* me," &c. " Lord, remember me " (Luke xxiii. 42). [4] (Wherewith) to restore.
[5] Penitence. [6] Lit., '' By help of it leap over the land," &c,

And then Repentance had pity and told them all to kneel. "For I will pray our Saviour for grace for all sinful ones, to heal us of our misdeeds, and have mercy on us all. Now, God," said he, "that of Thy goodness hast made the world, and of naught didst make aught and man most like Thyself; and then didst suffer him to sin—a sickness for us all, and all for the best, for I believe whatever the book telleth, *O felix culpa! O necessarium peccatum Ade,*[1] &c. For through that sin Thy Son was sent to the earth and became man of a maid, to save mankind, and didst make Thyself with Thy Son and us sinful ones alike. *Faciamus hominem ad ymaginem et similitudinem nostram.*[2]

Et alibi : qui manet in caritate, in deo manet, et deus in eo.[3] And afterwards, with Thy Son Himself, didst die in our flesh for man's sake on Good Friday, at full time of the day, and there Thyself nor Thy Son didst feel no sorrow in death, but in our flesh was the sorrow, and Thy Son took it, *Captivam duxit captivitatem.*[4] The sun for sorrow thereof lost his light for a time, about midday, the meal-time of saints,[5] when there is most light;

---

[1] O blessed sin ! O necessary sin of Adam !
[2] Let us make man in our image and our likeness.
[3] And elsewhere : Whoso dwelleth in love, dwelleth in God, and God in him.
[4] He led captivity captive.
[5] This expression seems to be a figurative one, having reference to the time of the crucifixion, when Christ's blood was

thou didst feed our forefathers in darkness with thy fresh blood, *Populus qui ambulabat in tenebris, vidit lucem magnam ;* [1] and through the light that went out of Thee Lucifer was blinded, and Thou didst blow [2] all Thy blessed into the bliss of Paradise. The third day after, Thou didst go about in our flesh, and sinful Mary alone saw Thee before St. Mary thy mother ; and all to solace the sinful Thou didst suffer it should be so. *Non veni vocare iustos, set peccatores ad penitenciam.* [3] And Thy bravest deeds, all that Mark, Matthew, John, and Luke, have written of, were done in our armour. [4] *Verbum caro factum est, et habitavit in nobis.* [5] And by so much, meseemeth, we may the more surely pray and beseech Thee, that art our Father and our Brother, if it be Thy will, be

shed upon the cross. It has also been suggested that there is reference here to Canticles i. 7. I prefer to take it in connection with the succeeding context, and to suppose that the poet is speaking of the crucifixion, as having been a time of refreshment to our forefathers who sat in darkness ; the force of which reference can only be understood by readers who are familiar with the apocryphal gospel of Nicodemus. There the quotation from Isa. ix. 2, is explained with reference to the " Harrowing of Hell," *i.e.,* the descent of Christ into hell to fetch out the souls of the Patriarchs. *(Skeat.)*

[1] The people who walked in darkness have seen a great light.

[2] The term "didst blow" is explained by the word " breath " used in a passage in the second part of the poem with regard to the entrance of Christ into hell, " with that breath hell brake open."

[3] I came not to call the just, but sinners to repentance.

[4] With our device upon his coat of arms. *(Skeat.)*

[5] The Word was made flesh, and dwelt amongst us.

merciful to us. And have pity on these sinners that here sorely repent them, that ever they angered Thee in this world in word, thought, or deeds."

Then Hope seized a horn of *Deus, tu conversus vivificabis nos,*[1] and blew it with *Beati quorum remisse sunt iniquitates,*[2] so that all the saints in heaven sang at once, *Homines et iumenta saluabis, quemadmodum multiplicasti misericordiam tuam, deus,*[3] &c.

And then thronged together a thousand men, who cried upward to Christ and His pure Mother for grace to go with them to seek Truth. But there was no man so wise among them who knew the way thither, and they wandered over banks and hills, groping, like beasts, for a long time, until it was late, when they met a man dressed as a Paynim in a pilgrim's guise. He bare a staff bound with a broad list, wound around it in the manner of bindweed.[4] A bowl and a bag he bare by his side ; a hundred ampulles[5] were placed upon his hat, tokens of Sinai, and shells of Galicia, and many a cross and keys-of-Rome on his cloak, and the vernicle in front so that men

[1] O God, thou hast converted us and wilt quicken us.
[2] Blessed are they whose iniquities are remitted.
[3] Thou wilt save man and beast (even) as thou hast multiplied thy mercy, O God.
[4] *I.e.*, wound round and round it like a creeping plant.
[5] These were little phials, containing holy water or oil, generally made of lead or pewter, nearly flat, and stamped with a device denoting the shrine whence they were brought. (*Skeat.*)

should know and see by his tokens whom he had sought.[1]

The people asked him first from whence he came.

"From Sinai," he said, "and from our Lord's sepulchre; I have been both in Bethlehem and Babylon, in Armenia, in Alexandria, and in many other places. Ye may see by my tokens on my hat that I have walked full far in wet and dry, and have sought good saints for my soul's health."

"Knowest thou aught of a saint that men call Truth? Couldest thou at all show us the way to his dwelling?"

"Nay, so God help me," said the man then, "I never saw palmer with staff or with scrip ask before about him, till now in this place."

"Peter!" said a ploughman, and thrust forward his head, "I know him as well as a clerk doth his books; Conscience and Mother-wit showed

[1] Besides the ordinary insignia of pilgrimage, every pilgrimage had its special *signs*, which "the pilgrim on his return wore conspicuously upon his hat or his scrip, or hanging round his neck, in token that he had accomplished that particular pilgrimage" (quoted from Cutt's "Scenes and Characters of the Middle Ages"). Thus the *ampullæ* were the special signs of the Canterbury pilgrimage; the scallop-shell was the sign of the pilgrimage to Compostella (shrine of St. James in Galicia); whilst the signs of the Roman pilgrimage were a badge with the effigies of St. Peter and St. Paul, the cross-keys (keys-of-Rome) and the vernicle. The *vernicle* was a copy of the handkerchief of St. Veronica, which was miraculously impressed with the features of our Lord. (*Skeat.*)

me his dwelling and made me promise faithfully
to serve him for ever both in sowing and planting,
as long as I could labour. I have been his follower all these fifty winters ; I have sown his
seeds and driven his beasts and looked after his
profit within and without. I ditch and I dig, and
I do what Truth biddeth ; sometimes I sow and
sometimes I thresh ; in tailors' or tinkers' craft
whatever Truth can devise ; I weave and I wind
and do what Truth biddeth. And though I say
it myself, I serve him to his pleasure. I have my
full hire from him and sometimes more. He is
the readiest payer that poor men know, he with-
holdeth from no man his hire when evening
comes. He is meek as a lamb and pleasant of
speech, and if ye wish to know where he dwelleth,
verily I will show you the way to his place."

"Yea, dear Piers," said these pilgrims, and
proffered him hire to go with them to Truth's
dwelling-place.

"Nay, by my soul's health," said Piers, and
began to swear, "I would not take a farthing for
St. Thomas' shrine ! Truth would love me the
less a long time after ; but if ye wish indeed to go,
this is the way thither that I shall tell you and set
you on the true road.

"Ye must go through Meekness, both men and
women, until ye come into Conscience, let Christ
know the truth, that ye love our Lord God the
best of all things ; and then in no wise hurt your

neighbour any more than thou wouldest he should thyself.

" And so turn forth by a brook, Be-humble-of-speech, till ye find a ford, Honour-your-Fathers, *Honora patrem et matrem,*[1] &c. Wade in that water, and wash you well there, and ye shall all your life go the more easily. And then thou shalt see Swear-not-at-all-except-it-be-of-need-and-in-special-not-idly-by-the-name-of-God-Almighty. Then thou shalt come by a croft, but go not therein ; that croft is called Covet-not-men's-goods-nor-their-wives-nor-any-of-their-servants-to-vex-them. See that ye break no boughs there except they be your own. Two stocks stand there, they are called Steal-not and Slay-not, but tarry not, strike forth past both and leave them on thy left hand and look not thereafter ; and keep well thy holiday till even.

" Then shalt thou turn away from a hill, Bear-no-false-witness ; it is hedged in with florins and many other fees : see thou pluck no plant there, for the peril of thy soul.

" Then shalt thou see Say-truth-as-it-is-to-be-done-in-no-other-manner-for-any-man's-bidding.

" Then shalt thou come to a court as bright as the sun ; the moat about the manor is of Mercy, and all the walls are of Wit to keep Will out, and embattled with Christendom to guard mankind, and buttressed with Believe-so-or-thou-shalt-not-

[1] Honour father and mother, &c.

be-saved. And all the houses, the halls and the chambers, are covered not with lead, but with Love and Lowly-speech-like-brethren.

"The bridge is of Pray-well-and-the-better-mayst-thou-speed ; each pillar is of Penance of prayers to saints, and of alms-deeds are the hinges that the gates hang upon. The porter is called Grace, a good man forsooth ; his man is called Amend-you for many a man knoweth him ; say to him this sign that Truth may know the truth, ' I performed the penance the priest enjoined me and am full sorry for my sins, and so I shall ever be when I think thereon, though I were a pope.'

" Pray Amend-you then to humble himself to his master, and to ask him to lift up the wicket that the woman shut, when Adam and Eve ate un-roasted apples. *Per Evam cunctis clausa est, et per Mariam virginem iterum patefacta est ;* [1] for he hath the keys and the latch, though the King may sleep.

"And if Grace grant thee to go in in this wise thou shalt see Truth dwelling in thy heart in a chain of charity, even as if thou wert a child to suffer him and say naught against thy Father's will. But then beware of Wrath, who is a wicked shrew ; he hath envy towards Him who dwelleth in thy heart ; and thrusteth forth Pride, for praise of thyself. The boldness of thy good deeds then

---

[1] By Eve it was shut to all, and by Mary the Virgin it was opened again.

maketh thee blind, and then thou shalt be driven out as dew and the door closed, and keyed and latched to keep thee out ; haply a hundred winters before thou enter again. Thus thou mightest lose his love for setting much by thyself, and haply never enter again, except thou have grace.

"But there are seven sisters who serve Truth ever, and they are porters of the posterns, and belong to the place. One is called Abstinence, and another Humility, Charity and Chastity are his chief handmaids, Patience and Peace help much people, Largess the lady hath let in full many. She hath helped a thousand out of the devil's pinfold. And whoso is akin to these seven, so God help me, he is wondrously welcome and received kindly. And except ye be akin to some of these seven, it is full hard, by my head," said Piers, " for any one of you to get entrance at any gate there, except there be more grace."

"Now, by Christ," said a cutpurse, "I have no kin there."

"Nor I," said an ape-keeper, "for aught I know ! "

"God save us," said a wafer-seller, " if I knew this for truth I would go never a foot further for any friar's preaching."

"Yes, verily," said Piers the Plowman, and egged them all on to goodness, " Mercy is a maiden there who hath power over them all ; and she is akin to all the sinful, and her Son also ;

and through the help of those two (hope thou none other), thou mightest find favour there, if thou go betimes."

" By St. Paul," said a pardoner, " peradventure I be not known there ; I will go fetch my box with my brevets, and a bull with bishop's letters ! "

" By Christ," said a low woman, " I will follow thy company ; thou shalt say I am thy sister ; I know not where they may come to ! " [1]

[1] The C-text adds here : Yea, *villam emi* [I have bought a farm]," said one, " and now I must thither to see how it pleaseth me," and took his leave of Piers. Another right anon said he " must needs follow five yoke [of oxen], therefore it behoveth me to go with a good will and quickly drive them. Therefore, I pray you, Piers, peradventure if ye meet Truth, ask that I may be excused." Then was there one called Active, he seemed a husband. "I have wedded a wife," he said, " of right wanton ways ; were I a se'nnight from her she would sin, and lour on me, and chide me lightly, and say I love another. Therefore, Piers Plowman, I pray thee say to Truth I may not come, for a Kit she clingeth to me so." . . . Said Contemplation, "Though I suffer sorrow, famine, and want, I will follow Piers."

Piers the Plowman is to go with the pilgrims to find Truth, but has first to plough a piece of land—He gives them all good advice and makes his will—He sets the pilgrims to work— Many are idle, but Hunger subdues them—Hunger then counsels Piers, and refuses to go away—The people have to feed him.

"THIS way were hard to find except we had a guide who would go with us every step." Thus this folk complained.

Said Perkin the Plowman, " By St. Peter of Rome, I have a half-acre to plough by the high-way, if I had ploughed and planted this half-acre I would go with you and show you the way."

"That would be a long tarrying," said a lady in a veil. "What should we women work at mean-while ? "

" Some shall sew the sack," said Piers, " to keep the wheat from spilling; and, ye lovely ladies, with your long fingers, who have silk and sendal to sew, make, while ye have time, chasubles for chaplains to adorn churches. Wives and widows, spin ye wool and flax, make cloth, I counsel you,

9

and so teach your daughters. Take heed how the needy and the naked lie, and devise clothes for them, for so Truth commandeth. For I will give them their livelihood unless the land fail, flesh and bread both for rich and poor as long as I live, for the Lord of Heaven's love. And all manner of men who live by meat and drink, help them to work busily who win your food."

" By Christ," then said a knight, " he teacheth us the best, but about that matter, truly, I was never taught. But teach me," said the knight, " and, by Christ, I will try ! "

" By St. Paul," said Perkin, " ye proffer yourself so fairly that I will swink and sweat and sow for us both, and do other labours for thy love all my life, in covenant that thou keep Holy Church and myself from wasters and from wicked men who spoil this world. And go hunt boldly for hares and foxes and boars and badgers that break down my hedges, and go tame the falcons to kill wild fowl ; for they come to my croft and crop my wheat."

Then the knight said courteously, " I pledge my faith, Piers, to fulfil this covenant after my power, though I should fight for it ; as long as I live I will uphold thee."

" Yea, and yet one more point I pray you," said Piers. " See that ye vex no tenant, except Truth will assent. And though ye may amerce them, let Mercy be the taxer, and Meekness thy master in spite of Meed's checks ; and though poor men offer you presents and gifts, take it not lest ye may not deserve it ; for thou shalt pay for it again at a year's end, in a dreadful place called ✓ Purgatory. And if thou ill-use not thy bondmen thou mayst speed the better ; though he be here thine underling, in heaven it may well hap that he be set higher and in greater bliss than thou, except thou do better and live as thou shouldst ; *Amice, ascende superius.* [1] For in the charnel-house at the church it is hard to know churls, or a knight from a knave ; know this in thy heart. And see thou be true of tongue and do thou hate tales, except they be of wisdom or wit, to chasten thy workmen. Hold with no ribalds nor listen to their lies, and specially at meals eschew such men ; for they are the Devil's story-tellers, I bid thee understand."

" I assent, by St. James," then said the knight, " I will do according to thy words while my life lasteth." *= Piers*

" And I will clothe me," said Perkin, " in a pilgrim's guise, and I will go with you till we find Truth, and I will put on me my clothes which are patched and full of holes, my leggings,[2] and my

[1] Friend, go up higher.
[2] *Cockers* (orig.), " a casing for the leg ; applied at various times to a kind of legging, a highlaced boot, or a combination of boot and legging, worn by husbandmen, hunters, fishers, &c., to protect the legs. The word is still used in the North for gaiters or leggings, and even for coarse stockings without feet, used as gaiters (called in Scotland *loags*)." (*New English Dictionary.*)

cuffs against the cold in my nails, and hang my seed-basket at my neck instead of a scrip, and put therein a bushel of bread-corn ;[1] for I will myself sow it, and then I will go on a pilgrimage to get pardon, as palmers do. But whoso now will help me to ear or to sow before I set out, by our Lord he shall have leave to glean here in harvest time, and make merry therewith in spite of any who may grudge it. And every kind of craftsman who can live honestly and faithfully I will find them food ; but not Jack the juggler and Janet of the stews and Daniel the dice-player and Denot the bawd, nor the lying friar and the folk of his order, nor Robin the ribald, because of his foul words. Truth once told me and bade me repeat it, *Deleantur de libro viventium.*[2] I must not deal with them ; for Holy Church is commanded to take no tithe of them, *Quia cum iustis non scribantur;*[3] by good luck they have escaped payment, now God amend them ! "

Piers's wife is called Dame Work-while-time-is, and his daughter Do-right-or-thy-mother-will-beat-thee ; his son is named Suffer-thy-sovereigns-to-have-their-will-judge-them-not-for-if-thou-dost-thou-shalt-dearly-abye-it.

---

[1] " Corn to be ground into *bread-meal* [*i.e.,* flour with only a portion of the bran taken out, from which brown bread is made] ; not to be used for finer purposes " (Peacock's glossary of certain Lincolnshire words, quoted by Skeat).

[2] Let them be blotted out from the book of the living.

[3] Because they are not written with the just.

" May God be with all," said Piers, " for thus His
word teacheth us.[1]

" For now I am old and hoary and have goods
of my own, I will go with the others in penance
and pilgrimage, and therefore, before I go, I will
write my bequest.

" *In dei nomine, amen,*[2] I will make it myself.
He shall have my soul who hath best deserved it,
and He will defend it from the devil, as I believe,
till I come before Him to His account, as my *Credo*
telleth me, to have release and remission on that
rental,[3] I hope. The Church shall have my body
and keep my bones, for he [4] asked the tithe on my
corn and my goods, and I readily paid it lest my
soul should be in peril, therefore he is bound, I
hope, to put me in his Mass and mention me
among all Christians in the Commemoration.[5]

" My wife shall have what I earned honestly and
no more, and share it with my daughters and my
dear children. And though I should die to-day
my debts are all paid ; I took home what I had
borrowed before I went to bed. And with the

---

[1] C. inserts, amongst others, the following lines : " That
which lords, such as mayors and senators, command us as
from the King oppose it never ; all that they command, I bid
thee verily that thou suffer it ; work thou after their warning and
words, but after their doing do thou not, my dear son," quoth
Piers.

[2] In the name of God, amen.

[3] *I.e.*, a release from the dues recorded in the rental.

[4] *He*, refers to the *persona ecclesiæ*, the parson. (*Skeat.*)

[5] *I.e.*, Service for the dead.

residue and the remnant, by the Rood of Lucca,
I will honour Truth therewith, as I live, and be
his pilgrim at the plough for poor men's sake.
My plough foot shall be my pike-staff and pick
the roots apart,[1] and help my coulter to cut and
clean the furrows."

Now Perkin and his pilgrims have gone to
plough, and many helped him to ear this half-acre.
Ditchers and delvers digged up the balks, and
Perkin was pleased therewith, and praised them
much.   Other workmen there were who worked
full eagerly, each man in his own way made himself busy, and some, to please Perkin, digged the
weeds up.   At high prime[2] Piers let the plough
stand, that he might look after them ; and whosoever worked best he should be hired afterwards
when the harvest-time should come.

And then some were sitting and singing at the
ale, and helping to ear his half-acre with " How
trollilolli ! "

" Now by peril of my soul," said Piers, in pure
anger, " except ye arise quickly and hasten to
work, no grain that groweth shall gladden you
in your need, and though ye die for grief, the
devil take him that careth ! "

Then were the rogues afraid, and feigned to be

---

[1] The pike-staff means the pilgrim's spiked staff.   Piers says
that instead of carrying a pike-staff like a pilgrim, he will make
good use of his plough-foot, so as to push aside or pierce through
the roots that are in the soil.   (*Skeat.*)

[2] Nine o'clock a.m.

blind ; some twisted [1] their legs as such rascals
can, and made their moan to Piers and prayed
mercy of him. " For we have no limbs to labour
with, Lord, thanked be ye ; but we pray for you,
Piers, and also for your plough, that of His grace
God may multiply your grain, and repay you for
your alms that ye give us here, for we may not
swink nor sweat, such sickness aileth us."

" If what ye say be true," said Piers, " I shall
soon find it out ! Ye are wasters, I know well,
and Truth knoweth the truth ! And I am his old
servant, and am bidden warn him who they are
in the world who have harmed his workmen. Ye
waste what men earn by travail and trouble, but
Truth shall teach you to drive his team ere ye shall
eat barley-bread and drink of the brook. But if
one be blind or broken-legged or fettered with
irons, he shall eat wheat-bread and drink with
me, till God in His goodness send him a remedy.

" But ye could work as Truth wished, and get
meat and hire for keeping cows in the field and
the corn from the beasts ; ye could ditch or delve
or thresh the sheaves, or help to make mortar,
or carry muck a-field. In lechery and lying and
sloth ye live, and it is all through long-suffering
that vengeance doth not overtake you. But
anchorites and hermits, who only eat at noon,
and no more till the morrow, they shall have

---

[1] The original word is *aliri* = across (?) or perhaps "loosely
stretched out." The men were shamming lameness.

my alms, and my goods shall clothe those who have cloisters and churches. But Robert Runabout shall have nought of mine, nor shall any apostles,[1] except they can preach and have power from the bishop ; these may have bread and pottage and be at ease, for it is an ill-ruled Order that hath nothing to depend upon."

Then a waster grew angry and would have fought, and offered his glove to Piers the Ploughman. A Britoner,[2] a braggart, thus also defied Piers :—

"Wilt thou or wilt thou not, we will have our will ; we will take thy flour and thy flesh when we like, and make us merry therewith, in spite of thy checks ! "

Then Piers the Plowman complained to the knight, to defend him, as their covenant was, from cursed shrews, and from these wolfish wasters, who harm the world. "For they waste and earn naught, and while that is there shall never be plenty among the people, as long as my plough standeth idle."

Then the knight courteously, as his habit was, warned Waster, and taught him better, "Or else, by mine Order, thou shalt abye it after the law ! "

"I was not wont to work," said Waster, "and I will not now begin ! " And he held Piers and

---

[1] *I.e.*, preachers.

[2] An inhabitant of Brittany, a Frenchman ; here a term of reproach. (*Skeat.*)

his plough but worth a pea, and threatened Piers and his men if they met again soon.

" Now by peril of my soul ! " said Piers, " I will punish you all ! " And he shouted for Hunger, who heard him at once. " Avenge me of these wasters, who shame the world," he said.

Then Hunger seized Waster quickly by the maw, and wrung him so that both his eyes watered ; he buffeted the Britoner about the cheeks so that he looked like a lantern ever afterwards. He beat them both so that he nigh broke their ribs ; and had not Piers with a peas-loaf prayed Hunger to cease, they had both been buried—deem thou naught else.

"Suffer them to live," he said, "and let them eat with hogs, or beans and bran baked together, or else milk and weak ale." Thus Piers prayed for them.

Canting rogues, for fear thereof, flew into barns, and flapped on with flails from morning till even, so that Hunger was not so bold as to look upon them.

For a potful of peas which Piers had got a crowd of hermits seized their spades, and cut up their cloaks and made short coats of them, and went as workmen with spades and shovels, and digged and ditched to drive Hunger away.

The blind and bedridden were bettered by the thousand, and those who sat begging silver were soon healed. For what was baked for a horse was good for many hungry men, and many a beggar was glad to work for beans, and every poor man was well pleased to have peas for hire, and what Piers asked them to do they did as quickly as a sparrow-hawk. And Piers was proud thereof, and put them to work[1] and gave them meat as he could afford, and a fair hire.

Then Piers had pity, and prayed Hunger to go home to his own land and stay there. "For I am now well avenged of wasters through thy might. But I pray thee before thou goest," said Piers to Hunger, "what is best to do with beggars and bidders? For I know well they will work full ill when thou hast gone; for misfortune has brought it about that they now are so meek, and only for want of their food are these men at my will."[2]

"They are my brethren by blood, for God bought us all," said Piers. "Truth once taught me to love every one of them and to help them always in all things as they needed it, and I would now learn of thee what it were best to do, how I could master them and make them work."

Then said Hunger, "Hear now, and hold it for wisdom: Big and bold beggars who can work for their bread do thou keep up their hearts with dogs' bread and horse bread; to bring down their

---

[1] C. adds: "At plastering, digging, bearing dung a-field, threshing, thatching, whittling of pegs."

[2] The C-text adds: "It is naught for love they thus labour steadfastly, but for fear of famine, in faith," said Piers. "There is no pure love with this folk, for all their fair speech."

bellies, stop their hunger with beans, and if the men murmur, bid them go work,[1] and they shall sup the sweeter when they have deserved it.

" And if thou find any whom fortune or any false men have injured, try to know them and comfort them with thy goods for Christ of Heaven's love. Love them and give to them as God's law teacheth: *Alter alterius onera portate.*[2] And all men thou canst espy who are needy and have naught, help them with thy goods, love them and blame them not, let God take vengeance ; though they do evil, let God be : *Michi vindicta, et ego retribuam.*[3] And if thou wilt be pleasing to God, do as the gospel teacheth, and make thyself beloved amongst lowly men, and so thou shalt find favour. *Facite vobis amicos de mamona iniquitatis.*"[4]

"I would not grieve God," said Piers, "for all the goods on earth ; might I do as thou sayest and be sinless ? "

" Yea ; I promise thee," said Hunger, " or else the Bible lieth. Go to Genesis the Giant, the beginning of us all. ' *In sudore*[5] and toil thou shalt earn thy meat, and labour for thy livelihood,' and thus our Lord bade. And Wisdom saith the same, I saw it in the Bible, ' *Piger pro frigore*[6] would till

---

[1] The pronoun in the original changes here to singular.
[2] Let each bear the burdens of the other.
[3] Vengeance is mine, and I will repay.
[4] Make to you friends of the mammon of unrighteousness.
[5] In sweat.
[6] The sluggard for the cold.

no field, and therefore he shall beg and pray and no man shall abate his hunger.' Matthew with a man's face [1] said these words, that *servus nequam* [2] had a talent, and because he would not trade with it he had his master's ill-will for ever more. And because he would not work his lord took the talent from him, and gave it to him who had ten talents, and then, so that Holy Church might hear it, he said, ' He that hath shall have, and be helped when he needeth, and he that hath not, shall have naught, and no man shall help him ; and what he even thinketh to have I will take it from him.'

" Mother-wit would that every man should work either in ditching or digging or travailing in prayer ; Christ would that men should work either in contemplative life or active life. The Psalter saith in the Psalm of *beati omnes*, the man that feedeth himself by his faithful labour, he is blessed by the Book in body and soul. *Labores manuum tuarum,*" &c. [3]

" Yet I pray you," said Piers, " *par charite* [4] if ye know any line [5] of leechcraft, teach it me, my lord. For some of my servants, and myself also, work not for a whole week our belly acheth so."

" I wot well what sickness aileth you," said Hunger, " ye have eaten over much and that

---

[1] An allusion to a common representation of the evangelists, which likens Matthew to a *man*, Mark to a *lion*, Luke to a *bull*, and John to an *eagle*. (*Skeat.*)

[2] A wicked servant.　　　　[3] The labours of thy hands.

[4] For love.　　　　　　　　[5] Lit., *leaf.*

maketh you groan. But I bid thee, as thou dost wish thy health, that thou never drink before thou eatest somewhat. Eat not, I command thee, until Hunger take thee and send his sauce to savour thy lips, and keep some till supper time, and sit not too long, but rise up before Appetite have eaten his fill. Let not Sir Surfeit sit at thy board ; believe him not, for he is lecherous and dainty of tongue and his maw is ravenous for many meats.[1] And if thou diet thee thus I dare lay mine ears that Physic shall sell for food his furred hoods and his cloak of Calabria [2] with all the knobs of gold, and be glad, by my faith, to leave his physic and learn to labour on the land, for livelihood is sweet. For many leeches are murderers—Lord, amend them ! —they make men die through their drinks ere Destiny hath willed it."

"By Saint Paul, these are profitable words," said Piers. "Go now, Hunger, when thou wilt, fare thee well—for this is a fine lesson, the Lord repay it thee ! "

"I vow to God," said Hunger, "hence I will not go till I have both dined and drunk to-day."

[1] In the C-text the following lines, amongst others, are inserted here : "Remember Dives and Lazarus, and if thou hast the power, Piers, I counsel thee share thy bread, thy pottage, or thy relish, with all who beg at thy gate for food for God's love. Give them some of thy loaf though thou thyself chew the less. And though liars and thieves and idlers may knock, let them bide till the board be removed, but bear no crumbs to them till all thy needy neighbours have made their meal."

[2] A cloak trimmed with Calabrian fur.

" I have no penny," said Piers, " to buy pullets, nor geese, nor pigs, but I have two green cheeses, a few curds and cream, and an oat-cake, and two loaves of beans and bran baked for my children. And yet I say, by my soul, I have no salt bacon nor no eggs,[1] forsooth, to make collops, but I have parsley and leeks and many cabbages,[2] and eke a cow and a calf and a cart-mare to draw my dung a-field while the drought lasteth, and by this provision we must live till Lammastide ; and by that I hope to have harvest in my croft, and then may I get thy dinner, as it pleaseth me well."

All the poor people then fetched peascods, and brought in their laps beans and baked apples, onions and chervils and many ripe cherries, and offered this present to Piers, wherewith to please Hunger.

Hunger ate it all in haste and asked for more, and then the poor folk for fear fed Hunger quickly, with green leeks and peas, and they thought to poison him.   By that, harvest time drew nigh and new corn came to market.   Then the folk were glad, and fed Hunger with the best, with good ale as Glutton taught, and made him go to sleep.

[1] *Kokeney* : an egg ; the egg of the common fowl, hen's eggs ; or perhaps one of the small or misshapen eggs occasionally laid by fowls, still popularly called in some parts "cock's eggs," in German *hahneneier*.   The same word as " cockney," *i.e.*, egg of cocks (*New English Dictionary*).   Collops were made of eggs and bacon.

[2] Lit., cole-plant—any sort of cabbage.

And then Waster would not work, but wander about, and no beggar ate bread that had beans in it, but only bread of coket or clerematyn [1] or else of pure wheat ; nor in any wise would he drink any halfpenny ale, but the best and the brownest sold in the town.

Labourers that have no land to live on but their hands, deigned not to dine at morn on herbs a night old. No penny ale can please them nor any piece of bacon, but only fresh flesh or fish, fried or baked, and that *chaud* or *plus chaud* [2] against cold in their maw. And except he be hired at a high price he will complain and bemoan the time that he was made a workman. He talketh against Cato's [3] counsel, *Paupertatis onus pacienter ferre memento.* [4] He complaineth against God and grumbleth against Reason, and then he curseth the King and all his council for making such laws to vex labourers. But while Hunger was their master none of them would complain, nor strive against his statute, so sternly he looked upon them.

" But I warn you, workmen, earn while ye may ; for Hunger hasteneth fast hitherward, and shall awake to chastise wasters with water floods. Ere

[1] Fine kinds of white bread.
[2] Hot or hotter.
[3] Dionysius Cato ; the name commonly given to the author of a Latin work very popular in the Middle Ages, from which Langland here quotes.
[4] Remember to bear the burden of poverty patiently.

five years be fulfilled such famine shall arise, and
fruits shall fail through floods and foul weather,[1]
and thus said Saturn [2] and sent to warn you. When
you see the sun amiss and two monks' heads, and a
maid have the mastery and multiply by eight, then
shall the Death withdraw and Dearth be Justice,
and Daw the ditcher die for hunger, except God, in
His goodness, grant us a respite."[3]

[1] The original *foule wederes* = lit., bad storms; but the
nautical term "foul weather" is still in use with much the
same meaning.

[2] The evil influence of the planet Saturn was often thought to
bring disaster.

[3] One of the mysterious prophecies then popular. The
Death = the pestilence.

Truth sends Piers a bull of pardon—A Priest disputes its legality—The dispute awakens the Dreamer—A good life will be better than trust in indulgences at the Day of Doom.

TRUTH heard tell thereof and sent to Piers, and bade him take his teem and till the earth, and provided him a pardon, *a pena et a culpa*,[1] for him and his heirs for evermore. And he bade him stay at home and plough his fields ; and to all who helped him to plough, to plant, or to sow, or did any other service that could help Piers, Truth granted pardon with Piers Plowman.

I. Kings and knights who protect Holy Church, and rule the people in their kingdom righteously, have pardon to pass full easily through Purgatory, and to be companions with patriarchs and prophets in Paradise. [2] Holy bishops, if they be as they should be, advocates of both the laws,[2] and therewith preachers to the ignorant ; and inasmuch as they can amend the sinful, are peers with the apostles (this pardon showeth Piers), and in the Day of Doom shall sit at the high daïs.

[1] From temporal and eternal punishment.
[2] *I.e.*, duty to God and to men.

3 Merchants to the good had many years (remission of purgatory), but the Pope would grant none of them *a pena et a culpa*, because they keep not their holy days as Holy Church teacheth, and swear " By their soul," and " So God must help them,' against good conscience, so that they may sell their wares.

But Truth sent them a letter under his secret seal that they should buy openly what best pleased them, and afterwards sell it again and save the profit, and repair therewith *mesondieux*[1] and help sick folk, and busily mend bad roads and build up bridges that were all broken ; help maidens to marry or else make them nuns ; find food for prisoners and poor ; put scholars to school or to some other craft ; and help religious Orders and fix the rate of rent more fairly ;—" And I myself will send St. Michael, my archangel, that no devil shall injure you or affright you when you die. And I will guard you from despair if ye will do thus, and will send your souls safely to my saints in joy."

Then were the merchants glad, and many wept for joy and praised Piers the Plowman, who provided this bull.

4. The men of law who had pleaded for Meed had the least pardon, for the Psalter did not save such as take gifts, and especially from innocents who know no evil ; *Super*[2] *innocentem munera non*

---

[1] *I.e.*, houses of God—hospitals.   [2] See page 43.

accipies. Pleaders should take trouble to plead for
such and help them, and princes and prelates
should pay them for their labour, *A regibus et
pryncipibus eril merces eorum.*[1] But many a justice
and juror would do more for John[2] than *pro dei
pietale,*[3] believe thou naught else ! But he who
spendeth his speech and speaketh for the poor that
are innocent and needy and harm no man, and who
comforteth them in their ill-fortune without covet-
ing gifts, and for our Lord's love showeth the law
as he hath learned it, there shall no devil injure
him the least when he dieth, and he shall be safe
with his soul, as the Psalter beareth witness.
Domine, quis habitabit in tabernaculo tuo ?[4] &c.
But a sin is it to buy water or wind or wit or
fire the fourth ; for these four the Father of
Heaven made in common for the earth, and
these are Truth's treasures to help honest folk ;
they shall never wax or wane without God
Himself.

When they come to die who take from poor
men Meed for their pleading, and would have
indulgence, their pardon is full small at their
departure hence. Ye legists and lawyers hold
this true, and if I lie Matthew is to blame, for he
bade me write this to you, and told me this say-

---

[1] From kings and princes shall their reward be.
[2] Probably the image of St. John the Baptist on the coin ;
so = money. *Cf.* p. 33 " *Mouton,*" and p. 68 " *Cross.*"
[3] For the mercy of God.
[4] Lord, who shall dwell in Thy tabernacle?

ing *Quodcumque vultis ut faciant vobis homines, facite eis.*[1]

5. All labourers living who live by their hands, and take wage honestly and honestly earn, and live in love and under law, because of their lowly hearts, shall have the same absolution that was sent to Piers.

6. Beggars nor bidders are not in the bull, except the cause be honest which maketh them beg, for he who beggeth or asketh, except he have need, he is false like the devil and defraudeth the needy; and he also beguileth the giver against his will, who if he knew were not needy, would give to another more needy than he, and so would the neediest be helped. Cato and the clerk of the Stories[2] teach men thus; *Cui des, videto*[3] is Cato's teaching, and in the Stories he teacheth how to give thine alms: *Sit elemosina tua in manu tua donec studes cui des.*[4] But Gregory was a good man, and bade us give to all who ask, for His love who giveth to us all: *Non eligas cui miserearis ne, forte pretereas illum qui meretur accipere. Quia incertum est pro quo Deo magis placeas.*[5] For ye

---

[1] Whatsoever ye would that men should do to you, do ye to them.

[2] Probably Peter Comestor, who wrote the "Historia Scholastica," and died about 1198. (*Skeat.*)

[3] Consider to whom thou givest.

[4] Let thine alms be in thine hand until thou knowest to whom thou givest.

[5] Thou shalt not choose on whom thou wilt have pity, lest perchance thou pass by him who deserves to receive; for it is uncertain on behalf of whom thou mayest please God first.

know never who is worthy, but God knoweth who hath need. In him who taketh is the treachery, if there be any sin ; for he who giveth, payeth, and prepareth him for rest ; and he who beggeth, borroweth, and bringeth himself into debt. For beggars borrow evermore, and God Almighty is their surety to repay, and with usury thereto, them who give. *Quare non dedisti peccuniam meam ad mensam, ut ego veniens cum usuris exegissem illam ?* [1]

Therefore, beg not, ye beggars, except ye have great need ; for whoso hath wherewith to buy him bread, the Book beareth witness that he hath enough if he hath bread enough, though he have naught else : *Satis dives est, qui non indiget pane.* [2] Let your solace be in reading saints' lives. The Book forbiddeth beggary, and blameth it in this manner : *Junior fui, etenim senui ; et non vidi iustum derelictum, nec semen ejus querens panem.* [3] For ye beggars live in no love nor keep no law ; many of you wed not the women ye go with, but as wild beasts, neighing, are up and doing, and bring forth children that men call bastards. In their youth they break their back or some bone, and then ye for ever after go falsely begging with your children. There are more misshapen people

---

[1] Why didst thou not put out thy money at interest, so that at my coming I might have required it with ursury ?

[2] He is rich enough who lacks not bread. See p. 130 of Appendix for a passage in C-text.

[3] I have been young and now am old ; and I have not seen the just abandoned nor his seed begging their bread.

among these beggars than among all other kinds
of men who walk the earth.   And he who liveth
his life thus, when he goeth hence may loath the
time that ever he was made man.

But old and hoary men, who are helpless, and
women with child who cannot work, the blind and
the bedridden, and those with broken limbs,[1] who
take their mischance meekly, such as lepers and
others, shall have as full a pardon as the Plowman himself, for love of their lowly hearts our
Lord hath granted them their penance and purgatory here on earth.[2]

"Piers," then said a priest, "I must read thy
pardon, for I will interpret each clause and tell it
thee in English."

And Piers unfoldeth the pardon at his request,
and I, behind them both, beheld all the bull.   It
all lay in two lines, and not a leaf more, and was
written thus on Truth's witness :—

> " *Et qui bona egerunt, ibunt in vitam eternam,*
> *Qui vero mala, in ignem eternum.*" [3]

"Peter ! I can find no pardon," then said the

---

[1] C. adds here the following : "And all poor patient ones,
content with God's will, such as lepers, and poor folks fallen on
misfortune, such as prisoners, and pilgrims ; peradventure they
were robbed or slandered by evil men, and then lost their goods,
or have fallen into poverty through fire or flood."

[2] See Appendix, p. 134, for passage in C-text.

[3] And those who have done good shall go into life eternal,
and those who have done evil into everlasting fire.

✓

priest, "except ' Do well and have well, and God
shall have thy soul ; and do evil and have evil,
and hope thou no other but that after thy death-
day the devil shall have thy soul ! ' "

And Piers, for pure vexation, tore it in twain,
and said, *si ambulauero, in medio umbre mortis, non
timebo mala ; quoniam tu mecum es.*[1] " I shall
cease from my sowing," said Piers, "and labour
not so hard, no more be so busy for delighting of
my maw. Hereafter my plough shall be of
prayers and penance, and I will weep when I
should sleep, though wheat-bread should fail me.
The prophet ate his bread in penance and sorrow,
and by what the Psalter saith, so did many others ;
whoso loveth God faithfully his livelihood is full
easy. *Fuerunt michi lacrimi mee panes die ac nocte.*[2]
And, unless Luke lie, he teacheth us by the fowls
that we should not be too busy about the world's
bliss. *Ne solliciti sitis,*[3] he saith in the gospel ; and
to guide us showeth us examples. The fowls in
the field, who findeth them meat in winter ? They
have no garner to go to, but God provideth for
them all."

" What ! " said the priest to Perkin, " Peter !
methinketh thou art learned somewhat, who
taught thee thy book ? "

" Abstinence the Abbess taught me my A B C,"

[1] If I walk in the valley of the shadow of death, I will fear
no evil ; for thou art with me.

[2] My tears have been my bread day and night.

[3] Be not troubled.

said Piers, " and afterwards Conscience came and told me much more."

" Wert thou a priest, Piers," said he, " thou mightest preach where thou shouldst, as a divine in divinity, with *dixit insipiens*,[1] for thy theme."

" Ignorant fool," said Piers, " little dost thou look on the Bible, seldom dost thou behold Solomon's saws, *Eice derisores et iurgia cum eis, ne crescant*,[2] &c."

The priest and Perkin disputed one with the other, and because of their words I awoke, and looked about, and saw the sun then in the south ; meatless and moneyless, on Malvern Hills, and musing on this dream, I went my way.

Many a time this dream hath made me ponder concerning what I saw asleep, whether it might be so ; and also, full pensive of heart, concerning Piers the Plowman, and what kind of pardon Piers had to comfort all the people, and how the priest impugned it through two special words. But I have no pleasure in divination of dreams, for I see it often fail.

Cato and canonists counsel us to cease to put faith in divination of dreams, for *sompnia ne cures*.[3]

But yet the book Bible beareth witness how Daniel divined the dreams of a king, who was

---

[1] The fool hath spoken.
[2] Cast forth scorners, and contentions with them, lest they increase.
[3] Heed not dreams.

called by clerks Nebuchadnezzar. Daniel said, "Sir King, thy dream betokens that strange knights shall come to cleave thy kingdom ; among lower lords than thou thy land shall be divided." And as Daniel divined, so afterward indeed it befell, and the king lost his lordship and lower men had it.

And Joseph dreamed marvellously how the moon and the sun and the eleven stars all made to him obeisance. Then Jacob declared Joseph's dream : "*Beau filtz,*"[1] said his father, "for want we shall come, and I, myself, and my sons, for need shall seek thee." It befell as his father had said, in the time of Pharaoh, that Joseph was Justice and governed Egypt, and his friends sought him there.

And all this maketh me think upon my dream. And how the priest found no pardon like Do-well,[2] and thought that Do-well surpassed indulgences, biennials and triennials,[3] and bishops' letters, and how Do-well shall be worthily received at the day of doom, and shall surpass all the pardon of St. Peter's Church.

Now the Pope hath power to grant the people pardon to pass into heaven without any penance. This is our belief, as learned men teach us. *Quodcumque ligaueris super terram, erit ligatum et in celis,*

[1] Fair son.

[2] *I.e.,* doing well, living a good life, here personified.

[3] Arrangements for saying mass for a departed soul during periods of two or three years. (*Skeat.*)

&c.[1] And so I truly believe (Lord forbid otherwise !) that pardon and penance and prayers cause indeed souls to be saved which have sinned deadly seven times. But to trust to these triennials, methinketh truly, is not so safe for the soul, certes, as is Do-well.

Therefore, I counsel you, ye men who are rich on this earth, and have triennials on trust of your treasure, be ye never the bolder to break the ten commandments ; and especially, ye masters, mayors, and judges, who are held for wise men, and have the wealth of this world and can purchase pardon and the Pope's bulls. At the dreadful Doom, when the dead shall rise and all come before Christ to yield account, how thou didst lead thy life here and didst keep His laws, and how thou didst do, day by day, the Doom will declare. A bagful of pardons there, or provincial letters, or though ye be found in the fraternity of all the four Orders, and have doublefold indulgences—except Do-well help you I set your patents and your pardons at the worth of a peashell ! Therefore I counsel all Christians to cry God mercy, and may Mary His mother be our mediator, that God may give us grace here before we go hence, to do such deeds while we are here, that after our death, at the Day of Doom, Do-well may declare we did as he bade.

[1] Whatsoever thou shalt bind on earth shall be bound also in heaven.

APPENDICES.

115

A

(See Page 35.)

"Though they give them dishonest measure they hold it no fraud ; and though they fill not full the measure sealed by law[1] they grasp for it as much as for the true measure.

"Many sundry sorrows often hap in cities, both through fire and flood, and all because of dishonest men who beguile good men and vex them wrongly ; and these cry on their knees for Christ to avenge them, either here on earth, or in hell, upon those who cheat them of their goods. And God sendeth upon them fevers, or fouller evils, or fire in their houses, or murrain, or other misfortune ; and it befalleth many a time that Innocence is heard in heaven among the saints, who pray both to our Lord and our Lady to grant these deceivers grace to amend on earth, and to have

---

[1] This alludes to the sealing or marking of measures, to insure their being true. (*Skeat.*)

117

their penance on earth and not in the torment of hell.

"And then there falleth fire on false men's houses, and for their sins good men burn in the fire. All this we have seen when sometimes, through a brewer, many houses are burned and the dwellers in them ; and because of a candle guttering in an evil place, which fell down and straightway burnt up all the row.

"Therefore, methinketh that mayors who make freemen ought to ask and find out, in spite of any word of silver, what manner of trade or merchandise such an one may use before he be made free and fellow on your rolls. Forsooth, it is not seemly, either in city or borough, that usurers or retailers, for any kind of bribe, be franchised and made free men and bear a false name."

[C. Passus iv. ll. 87–114.]

(*See Page* 40.)

"But I saved myself and sixty thousand lives, both here and elsewhere, in every land. But, if any durst say it, thou thyself, truly, hast made dull the heart of many bold men who had will to fight —to burn, and break in pieces, and beat down strongholds.

"In the lands whither the King went Conscience hindered him, so that he felled not his foes, though Fortune willed it, and as his destiny was ordained by our Lord's will.

"Like a caitiff, thou, Conscience, didst counsel the King to leave his heritage of France in his enemy's hand. Unwise is that conscience which sells a kingdom that is conquered through the help of all ; a kingdom or duchy may verily not be sold, for so many folk who fought for it and followed the King's will, ask their share of it. The least lad who followeth him, if the land be won, looketh for lordship or some other large Meed, whereby he may live ever after as befitteth a man. And that is the manner of a king who conquereth his enemies—to provide well for all his host or else to grant his men all that they can win, therewith to do what they best would. Therefore I counsel no king to ask any counsel of Conscience, if he desire to conquer a realm ; for never should Conscience be my constable, by Mary, were I a crowned king," said Meed, "nor be marshal of my men where I must fight."

[C. Passus iv. ll. 234-258.]

(*See Page* 42.)

"There is no man living who loveth not Meed, and is not glad to seize her, whether great lord or poor man." . . .

Said Conscience to the King, . . . "There is Meed and Mercede [1] and men deem both their due for certain deeds, secret or otherwise. Oftentimes men give Meed before the thing is done, and that

---

[1] Mercede = wages due for work actually done. (*Skeat.*)

is neither reason nor right, nor law in any realm, that a man should take Meed except he deserve it ; nor to undertake to work for another while he wotteth not verily whether he may live so long, nor have good hap in his health to earn Meed.

" I hold him over-bold, or else not honest, who is paid *pre manibus*,[1] or else asketh it. Harlots and false leeches ask their wage ere they have earned it. And deceivers give beforehand, and good men at the end, when the deed is done and the day ended, and that is no Meed, but Mercede, and a kind of debt due for the doing."

[C. Passus iv. ll. 283, &c.]

(See Page 56.)

" But, Reason, be thou my chief Chancellor in Exchequer and in Parliament, and Conscience be King's Justice in all my Courts."

" I assent," said Reason, " if so be that thou thyself hear, *audi alteram partem*[2] among aldermen and commoners ; and so that unfitting Sufferance[3] seal not your private letters, nor send *supersedeas*, except I assent. And I dare lay my life that Love will give the silver to pay the hire of thy servants, and help to get what thou dost desire, more than all thy merchants or thy mitred bishops, or Lombards of Lucca, who live by lending like Jews."

[1] Beforehand.
[2] Hear the other side.
[3] *I.e.*, " fraudulent connivance."

The King then commanded Conscience to send away all his officers and to receive those that Reason loved ; and right with that I waked.

[C. Passus v. ll. 185–196.]

(See Page 56.)

Thus I awaked, God wot, when I dwelt on Cornhill, Kit and I in a cottage ; clothed like a loller[1] and little set by, in sooth, believe me, among lollers of London and ignorant hermits, for I wrote verse of these men as Reason taught me. For as I came by Conscience I met with Reason, in a hot harvest-time, when I had my health, and limbs to labour with, and loved to fare well and do nothing but drink and sleep ; thus in health of body and wholeness of mind, one then questioned me ; roaming through remembrance, thus Reason rebuked me :—

" Canst thou serve or sing in a church," he said, " or cock hay for my harvest men, or pitch it in the cart, mow or stack it, or bind into sheaves, reap, or be a master-reaper and arise early, or have a horn and be a hedge-warder,[2] and lie out at nights and keep my corn in my croft from plunderers and thieves? Or make shoes or clothes, or keep sheep or kine, hedge or harrow, or drive swine or geese, or follow any other craft that the folk in common need to provide livelihood for the bedridden ? "

[1] A lounger, an idle vagabond.
[2] One who had to see that the cattle were kept within their right boundaries.

11

"Certes," I said, "and so God help me, I am too weak to work with sickle or scythe, and too long, believe me, to stoop low to work as a workman, for any length of time."

"Then hast thou lands to live by," said Reason, "or rich kindred who find thy food? For thou seemest an idle man, a spender that must spend, or a waster of time, or beggest thou about for thy living at men's doors, or in churches upon Fridays or feast-days? The which is a loller's life, little praised where righteousness giveth reward according as men earn it, *reddit unicuique iuxta opera sua.*[1] Or thou art injured, maybe, in body or in limb, or maimed through some mishap, whereby thou mayest be excused?"

"When I was young," I said, "many years ago, my father and my friends found wherewith to school me, till I knew assuredly what Holy Writ meant, and what is best for the body, and most safe for the soul, as the Book telleth, if so be that I continue it. And yet since my friends died I never found, forsooth, a life that pleased me except in these long robes. If I must live by labour and earn a livelihood, that labour that I learned best, thereby must I live. *In eadem vocatione in qua vocati estis, manete.*[2] And I live both in London and upon London; the tools with which I work and earn a living are *paternoster* and my primer

[1] He renders to every one according to his works.
[2] In the same calling wherein ye have been called, abide.

placebo and *dirige*, and sometimes my Psalter and my Seven Psalms. Thus I sing for the souls of such as help me, and those who find me my food, undertake, I trow, to make me welcome when I come at times in a month, now to him and now to her ; and in this manner I beg without bag or bottle, save my maw only. And also moreover, methinketh, Sir Reason, men should constrain no clerk to the work of knaves, for by the law of *Levitici* that our Lord ordained, clerks that are crowned[1] by conscience[2] should neither labour nor sweat, nor swear at inquests, nor fight in the van nor grieve their foes ; *non reddas malum pro malo.*[3] For all who are crowned are heirs of heaven, and in the choir or in churches are Christ's own ministers. It becometh clerks to serve Christ, and uncrowned knaves to drive the cart and to work. For no clerk should be crowned except he come of franklins and free men and of wedded folk. Bondmen and bastards and beggars' children, to these it belongeth to labour ; and to the Lord's kindred to serve both God and good men, as their degree requireth ; some to sing Masses, or sit and write, to advise and to receive what Reason ought to spend. But since bondmen's sons have been made bishops, and bastards' off-spring have been archdeacons, and soap-dealers

[1] *I.e.*, tonsured.
[2] Lit., *kynde understondyng—i.e.*, the inner voice which prompted the choice of the life of a clerk.
[3] Render not evil for evil.

and their sons have been made knights for silver ; and lords' sons their labourers, and their revenues laid in pledge for the right of the realm to ride against our enemies, for the Commons' comfort and the King's honour ; and monks and nuns who should provide for beggars have made knights of their kindred and purchased knight fees—popes and patrons refuse poor gentle blood, and choose Simon's son [1] to keep the sanctuary. Holy living and love have been long hence, and will be till this be worn out or otherwise changed.

"Therefore, rebuke me right naught, Reason, I pray you, for in my conscience I know what Christ would that I should do. The prayers of an upright man and discreet penance is the best labour to please our Lord. *Non de solo*," I said, "forsooth, *vivit homo, nec in pane et pabulo* [2] the *paternoster* witnesseth ; *fiat voluntas tua* [3] findeth us all things."

Said Conscience, "By Christ I cannot see how this applieth, but it seemeth not uprightness to beg in cities, except one be Obediencer [4] to priory or minster."

"That is true," I said, "and so I confess that I have lost and misspent time ; and yet I hope, as he that oft hath chaffered and aye hath lost and lost, and at last it hath happened him that he made

---

[1] That is, the son of Simon Magus, or one who has been guilty of Simony—whose wealth was his recommendation. (*Skeat.*)

[2] Not alone by bread and meat man liveth.

[3] Thy will be done.   [4] A certain officer in a monastery.

such a bargain that he was ever after the richer, and at the end set his loss at a leaf's worth, such a winning was it to him by the words of His grace; *Simile est regnum celorum thesauro abscondito in agro*, &c. : *Mulier que invenit dragmam unam*, &c. ;[1] even so I hope to have from Him who is almighty a share of His grace, and begin a time that will turn all the times of my time to profit."

"I counsel thee, then," said Reason, "haste thee to begin the life that is worthy and honest for the soul."

"Yea, and continue it," said Conscience ; and to the church I went.

To the church I went to honour God, and before the cross on my knees I knocked my breast, sighing for my sins, saying my *paternoster*, and weeping and wailing till I was asleep.

[C. Passus vi. ll. 1–108.]

(See Page 59.)

Gregory the great clerk bade write in books the rule for all religious Orders which were righteous and obedient. Even as fishes in the flood, when water faileth them die for drought when they lie dry, so a religious Order rotteth and dieth that coveteth to dwell outside convent and cloister. For if heaven be on this earth or any ease for the soul, it is in cloister or school, I find, for many

---

[1] The kingdom of heaven is like to a treasure hid in a field, &c. [See also concerning] The woman who found the drachma.

reasons. For in cloister no man cometh to chide
or fight, and in school there is lowliness and love
and liking to learn. But many a day men tell that
both monks and canons have ridden out in array
and kept their rule ill, and have been leaders of
love-days, and have purchased lands, and ridden
about on palfreys from mansion to manor, a pack
of hounds at his back as if he were a lord. And
except his knave kneel who holdeth his cup, he
looketh scowling and calleth him "lordein." [1]
Little had lords to do to give lands away from their
heirs to religious Orders, who have no ruth, though
it rain on their altars. In mansions where these
parsons are at ease by themselves no pity have
they on the poor ; that is their pure charity. Ye
all hold yourselves lords, your land lieth too wide.
But yet there shall come a king and confess you
all, and beat you for breaking your rule, as the
Bible telleth ; and put you to your penance *ad
pristinum statum ire.* [2] Barons and their offspring
shall blame and reprove you ; *Hii in curribus et hi
in equis : ipsi obligati sunt, et ceciderunt.* [3] Friars
in their refectory shall find in that time bread
without begging, to live by ever afterwards, and
Constantine [4] shall be their cook and the restorer

---

[1] Lazy villain.   [2] To return to the first condition.
[3] Some (trust) in chariots and some in horses; they are
brought down and have fallen.
[4] It was a legend of the Middle Ages that Constantine
bestowed his territory in Italy upon the Pope. This passage
"seems to look forward to a time when the friars should be sup-
ported by some kind of regular endowment."

of their churches. For the Abbot of England[1] and the Abbess, his niece, shall have a knock on their crowns, and incurable shall be the wound ; *contriuit dominus baculum impiorum virgam domi-nancium plaga in-sanabili.*[2] But ere that king come, as Chronicles have told me, clerks and Holy Church shall be clothed anew."

[C. Passus vi. ll. 147–180.]

(See Page 60.)

" I, Pride,[3] patiently ask penance, because foremost and first I have been disobedient to father and mother ; and disobedient and not abashed to offend God and all good men, so high was my heart ; disobedient to Holy Church and to them who served there. I judged some for their evil vices, and excited others through my word and my wit to show their evil works : and scorned them and others if I found a reason, laughing all aloud so that unlearned men should ween that I was cleverer and wiser than another ; a mocker and unreasonable to them who showed reason, in

---

[1] Another reading for "England" is "Abingdon." At Abingdon there was an old and well-known abbey. "It was the house into which the monks, strictly so called, were first introduced into England, and is, therefore, very properly, introduced as the representative of English monachism." (*Skeat.*)

[2] The Lord hath broken the staff of the wicked, the rod of the rulers, with an incurable stroke.

[3] This addition to the B-text gives a second example of Pride. Pernel Proudheart (in B, see p. 60) was a female character. Here, Pride is a man.

all kinds of ways, so that my name should be known ; seeming to be sovereign wheresoever it befel me to tell any tale, and I trowed me wiser to speak or to counsel than any clerk or layman. Proud of my apparel and my bearing among the people, more than I have reason for, within or without ; wishing that men should ween I were, in what I was, and had, rich, eloquent, and righteous of life ; boasting and bragging with many bold oaths, vaunting in my vainglory in spite of any rebuke ; and, again, so much above all others in the people's sight that there was none such as myself nor none so pope-holy.[1]

"Sometime with one appearance, sometime with another ; in every covetous way I thus contrived a hundred times how I could be esteemed holy. I wished that men should think my deeds were the best, and I the most learned in my craft among clerks and others, and the strongest upon my steed, and the sturdiest in body, and the handsomest to look on, proud of my fair features and because I sang clearly. And what I gave for God's love I told to my friends, for them to think that I was right holy and full of almsgiving, and none else so bold a beggar to pray and to crave ; telling tales in taverns and streets, of things that were never thought, and yet I sware I saw them, and lied by both my body and my life. Of deeds that

[1] This is literal—holy as the Pope ; used here to mean hypocritical.

I did well I get witness, and say to such as sit beside me—" Lo ! if ye believe me not, or ye ween I lie, ask of him or of her, and they can tell you what I suffered and saw, and at some time had, and what I knew and could do, and what kin I came of."

[C. Passus vii. ll. 14–58.]

(See Page 62.)

All that he knew about Will he told it to Watkin, and all that he knew of Watkin he told it after to Will. And he made foes of friends through his false and faithless tongue, " Or through strong speech or many tricks I avenged me oft or fretted[1] myself within like a tailor's shears, and cursed my fellow Christians. . . . When I may not have the mastery I take such melancholy that I catch the çramp, and sometimes spasms ·of the heart, or the ague, in such a fit of anger ; and sometimes a fever that seizeth me for a whole twelvemonth, until I despise our Lord's leechcraft and trust in a witch and say that neither clerk nor Christ is skilled like the cobbler of Southwark, such grace is his. For God nor God's words, nor grace, never availed, but through a charm I have had good hap and my greatest healing.

[C. Passus vii. ll. 70–85.]

---

[1] I take here the reading " frete." " Envy fretted himself internally, just as the inner edges of a tailor's pair of shears grate against each other when used."

(See Page 70.)

With false words and tricks I have got my goods and with guile and deceit gathered what I have ; I mixed up my wares and made a good show, while the worst lay beneath, and I held it a fine trick. And if my neighbour had a hind, or any beast else, more profitable than mine, I contrived many plans, and cast about with all my wit how I might get it ; and except I got it by any other way, at last I stole it or privily shook his purse and unpicked his locks. And if I went to the plough I pinched a bit from his half-acre, so that I would steal away a foot of land or a furrow from my next neighbour's ground. And if I reaped I would over-reach, or gave counsel to them who reaped to seize for me with their sickle what I never had sowed, . . . and if I sent my servant over sea to Brugès, or my prentice into Prussia to look after my profit, to trade with money and make exchange, never could any man comfort me in the meantime, neither could Matins nor Mass, nor any other kind of show ; and I never performed penance nor said *paternoster* that my mind was not more with my goods than with God's grace and His great might.

[C. Passus vii. ll. 259–285.]

(See Page 109.)

The most needy are our neighbours if we take good heed, such as prisoners in dungeons or poor folk in cottages, burdened with children and the landlord's rent. What they save by their spinning they spend it in house-hire, also in milk and meal to make porridge with, to fill their children who cry for food. And they themselves suffer much hunger and woe in winter-time when they wake at nights to rise to rock the cradle, and also when they card and comb, and patch and wash and rub, and reel, and peel rushes, so that ruth is it to read or show in rime the woe of those women who dwell in cottages, as well as of any other men who suffer much woe, in hunger and thirst, that they may turn the fair side outward ; and are abashed to beg, and would not tell to their neighbours what they need at noon and eve.

" Verily I know also, as the world teacheth, what befalleth another, who hath many children, and hath no wealth but his craft to clothe and feed them with, and many to grasp thereat, and who taketh few pence. Their bread and penny ale are taken instead of pittance,[1] and cold flesh and cold fish instead of baked venison. On Fridays and fasting days a farthing's-worth of mussels, or as many cockles, were a feast for such folk. It were alms to help those that have such burdens and to comfort such cotters, and crooked men and blind.

[1] A *pittance* at that time meant "an extraordinary allowance of victuals given to monastics in addition to their usual commons." (*Tyrwhitt*, quoted by Skeat.)

"But beggars with bags, whose churches are brew-houses, except they be blind or deformed or else sick, though they fall down for want that thus beg falsely for a living, reck them not, ye rich, though such rascals starve. For all that have their health and their eyesight, and limbs to labour with, and yet follow lollers' life, live against God's law and the teaching of Holy Church.

"And yet there are other beggars in health, it seemeth, both men and women, but they want their wit. And these are lunatic lollers and wanderers, mad, more or less, according as the moon sitteth. They care for no cold, nor take count of heat, and wander with the moon, and go moneyless and witless, with a good will, in many countries far and wide ; just as Peter and Paul did, except that they preach not nor do miracles. But many times it befalleth them to prophesy concerning the people, as it were in mirth. And in our sight, it seemeth since God has the might to give each man wit, wealth, and health, and yet suffereth these to go thus (it seemeth to my thinking), that such people are as His apostles, or His privy disciples, for He hath sent them forth silverless, and in a summer garment, without bread and bag as the book telleth, *Quando misi vos sini pane et pera ;* [1] barefoot and breadless they beg of no man. And though one may meet with the mayor in the

---

[1] When I sent you without bread and scrip.

street he reverenceth him right naught more than another ; *Neminem salutaueritis per viam.*[1] Such manner of men Matthew teacheth us we should take to house and help them when they come ; *Et egenos vagosque induc in domum tuam.*[2] For they are merry-mouthed men and minstrels of heaven, and are God's servants, jesters, as the Book telleth, *Si quis videtur sapiens, fiet stultus ut sit sapiens.*[3] Men know full well that it belongeth to the rich to receive all minstrels kindly, for the love of lords and ladies that they live with. Men suffer all that such say and take it for merriment, and do still more for such men, before they go, and give them gifts and gold for great lords' sakes. Right so, ye rich, ye should forsooth rather welcome and honour and help with your wealth God's minstrels and His messengers and His merry jesters, the which are lunatic lollers and wanderers, for under God's secret seal their sins are covered.

For they bear no bags nor bottles under their cloaks ; which belongeth to the life of lollers and of ignorant hermits who seem full humble to gain men's alms, in hope to sit at even by the hot coals, to spread abroad their legs or lie at their ease, to rest and roast and turn their back, to drink deep and dry, and then betake themselves

[1] Ye shall salute no man by the way.
[2] And the needy and wandering bring into thine house.
[3] If any seemeth wise, let him become a fool that he may be wise.

to bed and arise when it pleaseth them. When
they are risen they roam about and spy right well
where they may soonest have a meal or a round
of bacon, silver or sodden meat, and sometimes
both ; a loaf or half a loaf or a lump of cheese,
and carry it home to their cottage, and cast about
how to live in idleness and ease and by others'
travail.

And whatsoever man wandereth thus with a
bag at his back in beggar's guise, and knoweth
some kind of craft, in case he wished to use it,
through which craft he could come at bread and
ale, and, moreover, to a garment to cover his
bones and liveth like a loller—God's law damneth
him. "Lollers living in sloath and roamers over
the land are not in this bull," said Piers, "until
they amend them."

[C. Passus x. ll. 71–160.]

(*See Page* 110.)

But hermits that live by the highways, and in
towns among brewers, and beg in churches ;—
all that the holy hermits hated and despised, such
as riches, reverences, and rich men's alms, these
lollers, thieves, and worthless hermits covet the
contrary, and live as cotters. For they are but as
servants and drunkards at the alehouse, neither
of good lineage, nor learning, nor holy of life, as
hermits who of old dwelt in woods with bears
and lions. Some of these had livelihood from

their kindred and from no man else, and some
lived by their learning and the labour of their
hands ; some had strangers for friends who sent
them food, and to some birds brought bread
whereby they lived. All these holy hermits were
of noble kin, they forsook land and lordship and
the pleasures of the body.

But these hermits who build their dwelling by
the highway, of yore were workmen, weavers and
tailors and carters' knaves and graceless clerks.
They kept full hungry house and had much want,
long labour and little earning, and at last espied
that liars in friars' clothing had fat cheeks. Therefore these unlearned knaves left their labour and
clothed themselves in cloaks like clerks, or as if
they were of some Order, or else prophets . . .
Now, by Christ, rightly are such called "lollers,"
after the English of our elders, as old men teach.
He that lolleth is lame, or his leg out of joint, or
maimed in some limb, for it pointeth to some
mishap.

And even thus, truly, such manner of hermits
"loll" against the faith and law of Holy Church.
For Holy Church biddeth all manner of people to
be under obedience and submission to the law.
First, the Religious Orders, to keep their rule and
be under obedience day and night ; unlearned
men to labour ; and lords to hunt in woods and
forests for foxes and other beasts which are in
the wild woods and waste places, such as wolves

that worry men, women, and children. And all to cease on Sundays that they may hear God's service, both Matins and Mass ; and after meat ought every man to hear Evensong in churches.

Thus it behoveth to lord and clerk and layman, to hear the service wholly each holy-day, and furthermore to keep vigils and fasting days, and to fulfil those fastings, except infirmity should cause otherwise—poverty or other penances, such as pilgrimages and needful labour. Under this obedience are we each one ; whoso breaketh this, be well aware that except he repent, amend, and ask mercy, and humbly shrive himself, I fear me, if he die, it shall be counted for deadly sin before Christ, except Conscience excuse him.

Look now whether these lollers and ignorant hermits, who are so far from church, transgress this obedience ? Where see we them on Sundays hearing the service, such as Matins in the morning ? Till Mass begin, or till Sundays at Evensong we see right few ! Or do they labour for their living as the law would ? But rather at midday meal-time oft I meet with him going in a cloak as if he were a clerk ; a bachelor or a holy father best beseemeth him ! And for the cloth that covereth him he is called a friar, and washeth and wipeth and sitteth with the first. But while he laboured in the world, and earned his meat with honesty, he sat at the side bench and second table, and no wine came into his belly through the week long, nor blanket in his bed nor white bread before him.

The cause of all this villainy cometh from many bishops who suffer such sots and other sins to rule. Certes, if one durst say it, *Symon quasi dormit ; vigilare* [1] were better, for thou hast a great charge. For many watchful wolves have broken into folds ; the barkers [2] are all blind who lead forth thy lambs, *dispergentur oues,* [3] thy dog dare not bark. The tar [4] is ill-made that belongeth to thy sheep, their salve is of *supersedeas* in summoners' boxes ; [5] nigh all thy sheep are scabbed, the wolf is surfeited with wool :—

"*Sub molli pastore lupus lanam cacat, et grex In-custoditus dilaceratur eo.*" [6]

Ho ! Shepherd ! where is thy dog and thy bold heart to fight the wolf that befouleth thy wool ? I believe that for thy sloth thou dost lose many wethers, and full many a fair fleece thou dost wash ill ! When thy lord looketh to have profit

---

[1] Simon sleeps as it were ; to watch.

[2] *I.e.,* dogs.

[3] The sheep shall be scattered.

[4] Every shepherd used to carry a tar-box, which held salve for anointing the sores of sheep.

[5] All the healing salve that the sheep get is that they are smothered with writs of *supersedeas.*

[6] Under a soft [yielding] shepherd the wolf casteth forth wool, and the unguarded flock is therefore torn in pieces.

for his beasts and for the money thou hadst wherewith to guard his goods, and the wool shall be weighed—woe is thee then !

[C. Passus x. ll. 188, &c.]

B

1. *The opening lines of the Prologue* (see p. 1).

In a somer seson · whan soft was the sonne,
I shope me in shroudes · as I a shepe were,
In habite as an heremite · unholy of workes,
˳Went wyde in þis world · wondres to here.
Ac on a May mornynge · on Maluerne hulles.
Me byfel a ferly · of fairy, me thou3te ;
I was very forwandred · and went me to reste
Under a brode banke · bi a bornes side,
And as I lay and lened · and looked in þe wateres,
I slombred in a slepyng · it sweyved so merye.

[Prol. ll. 1–10.]

2. *The rats and mice take counsel together to bell the cat* (see p. 8).

Wiþ þat ran þere a route · of ratones at ones,
And smale mys myd hem · mo þen a þousande,
And comen to a conseille · for here *comune* profit ;
For a cat of a courte · cam whan hym lyked,
And ouerlepe hem ly3tlich · and lau3te *hem* at his wille,
And pleyde wiþ hem perilouslych · and possed hem aboute.
' For doute of dyuerse dredes · we dar nou3te wel loke ;
And 3if we grucche of his gamen · he will greue vs alle,
Cracche vs, or clowe vs · and in his cloches holde,

---

[1] Edited by Prof. Skeat, Clar. Press 1891.

That vs lotheth þe lyf · or he lete vs passe.
Myȝte we wiþ any witte . his wille withstonde,
We myȝte be lordes aloft · and lyuen at owre ese.'
  A raton of renon · most renable of tonge,
Seide for a souereygne · help to hym-selue ; —
  ' I haue ysein segges,' quod he, · ' in þe cite of london
Beren biȝes ful briȝte · abouten here nekkes,
And some colers of crafty werk ; · vncoupled þei wenden
Boþe in wareine & in waste · where hem leue lyketh ;
And otherwhile þei aren elles-where · as I here telle.
Were þere a belle on here beiȝ · bi Iesu, as me thynketh,
Men myȝte wite where þei went · and awei renne !
  And riȝt so,' quod þat ratoun · ' reson me sheweth,
To bugge a belle of brasse · or of briȝte syluer,
And knitten on a colere · for owre comune profit,
And hangen it vp-on þe cattes hals · þanne here we mowen,
Where he ritt or rest · or renneth to playe.
And ȝif him list for to laike · þenne loke we mowen,
And peren in his presence · þer-while hym plaie liketh,
And ȝif him wratteth, be ywar . and his weye shonye '
  Alle þis route of ratones · to þis reson þei assented.
Ac þo þe belle was ybouȝt · and on þe beiȝe hanged,
Þere ne was ratoun in alle þe route · for alle þe rewme of
 · Fraunce
Þat dorst haue ybounden þe belle · about þe cattis nekke,
Ne hangen it aboute þe cattes hals · al Engelonde to wynne ;
And helden hem vnhardy · and here conseille feble,
And leten here laboure lost · & alle here longe studye.
                              [Prol. ll. 146–181.]

3. *The description of Meed* (see p. 21).

I loked on my left half · as þe lady me taughte,
And was war of a womman · wortheli yclothed,
Purfiled with pelure · þe finest vpon erthe,
Y-crounede with a corone · þe kyng hath non better.
Fetislich hir fyngres · were fretted with golde wyre,
And þereon red rubyes · as red as any glede,
And diamantz of derrest pris · and double manere safferes,
Orientales and ewages · enuenymes to destroye.
  Hire robe was ful riche · of red scarlet engreyned,
With ribanes of red golde · and of riche stones ;
Hire arraye me rauysshed · such ricchesse saw I neuere ;

I had wondre what she was · and whas wyf she were.
‘ What is þis womman,’ quod I ; ‘ so worthily atired ?’
‘ That is Mede þe Mayde,’ quod she, · ‘hath noyed me
    ful oft.’

[Passus ii. ll. 7–20.]

4. *From the confession of Avarice* (see p. 68).

‘ Repentedestow þe euere,’ quod repentance, · ‘ne restitu-
    cioun madest ?’
‘ Зus, ones I was herberwed,’ quod he, · ‘with a hep of
    chapmen,
I roos whan þei were arest · and yrifled here males.’
‘ That was no restitucioun,’ quod repentance, · ‘ but a
    robberes thefte,
Þow haddest be better worthy · be hanged þerfore
Þan for al þat · þat þow hast here shewed.’
‘ I wende ryflynge were restitucioun,’ quod he, · ‘for I lerned
    neuere rede on boke,
And I can no frenche in feith · but of þe ferthest ende of
    norfolke.’

[Passus v. ll. 232–239.]

5. *The Penitents’ search for St. Truth* (see p. 82).

A thousand of men þo · thrungen togyderes ;
Criede vpward to cryst · and to his clene moder,
To haue grace to go with hem · treuthe to seke.
    Ac þere was wyзte non so wys · þe wey þider couthe,
But blustreden forth as bestes · ouer bankes and hilles,
Till late was and longe · þat þei lede mette,
Apparailled as a paynym · in pylgrymes wyse.

   *   *   *   *   *

‘ Knowestow ouзte a corseint · þat men calle treuthe?
Coudestow auзte wissen vs þe weye · where that wy dwelleth?’
‘ Nay, so me god helpe !’ seide þe gome þanne,
‘ I seygh neuere palmere · with pike ne with scrippe,
Axen after hym er · til now in þis place.’
‘ Peter !’ quod a plowman · and put forth his hed,
I knowe hym as kyndely · as clerke doþ his bokes ;

Conscience and kynde witte · kenned me to his place,
And deden me suren hym sikerly · to serue hym for euere,
Bothe to sowe and to sette · þe while I swynke myghte.
I haue ben his folwar · al þis fifty wyntre ;
Bothe ysowen his sede · and sued his bestes,
With-Inne and with-outen · wayted his profyt.
I dyke and I delue · I do þat treuthe hoteth ;
Some tyme I sowe · and some tyme I thresche,
In tailoures crafte and tynkares crafte · what treuthe can
  deuyse,
I weue an I wynde · and do what treuthe hoteth.
 For þouȝe I seye it myself · I serue hym to paye ;
I haue myn huire of hym wel · and otherwhiles more ;
He is þe prestest payer · þat pore men knoweth ;
He ne with-halt non hewe his hyre · þat he ne hath it at euen.
He is as low as a lombe · and loueliche of speche,
And ȝif ȝe wilneth to wite · where þat he dwelleth,
I shal wisse ȝow witterly · þe weye to his place.'
     [Passus v. ll. 517–523 and 539–562.]

6. *Piers would dismiss Hunger, who refuses to go and has to be fed* (see p. 101).

' By seynt Poule,' quod pieres · ' þise aren profitable wordis !
Wende now, hunger, whan þow wolt · þat wel be þow euere !
For þis is a louely lessoun · lorde it þe forȝelde ! '
' Byhote god,' quod hunger, · ' hennes ne wil I wende,
Til I haue dyned bi þis day · and ydronke bothe.'
 ' I haue no peny,' quod peres, · ' poletes for to bigge,
Ne neyther gees ne grys · but two grene cheses,
A few cruddes and creem · and an hauer cake,
And two loues of benes and bran · ybake for my fauntis.
And ȝet I sey, by my soule · I haue no salt bacoun,
Ne no kokeney, bi cryst · coloppes for to maken.
Ac I haue percil and porettes · and many kole-plantes,
And eke a cow and a kalf · and a cart-mare
To drawe a-felde my donge · þe while þe drought lasteth.
And bi þis lyflode we mot lyue · til lammasse tyme ;
And bi þat, I hope to haue · heruest in my croft ;
And þanne may I diȝte þi dyner · as me dere liketh.'
Alle þe pore peple þo · pesecoddes fetten,
Benes and baken apples · þei brouȝte in her lappes,

Chibolles and cheruelles · and ripe chiries manye,
And profred peres þis present · to plese with hunger.
  Al hunger eet in hast · and axed after more.
Þanne pore folke fro fere · fedde hunger ȝerne
With grene poret and pesen · to poysoun hunger þei þouȝte.
By þat it neighed nere heruest · newe corne cam to chepynge ;
Þanne was folke fayne · and fedde hunger with þe best,
With good ale, as glotoun tauȝte · and gerte hunger go slepe.

                              [Passus vi. ll. 277–303.]